〔〕

B·W

Desert Justice

DESERT JUSTICE

M. E. MINER

III

W

cop. 4

AVALON BOOKS
THOMAS BOUREGY AND COMPANY, INC.
401 LAFAYETTE STREET
NEW YORK, NEW YORK 10003

PRINTED IN THE UNITED STATES OF AMERICA
BY HADDON CRAFTSMEN, SCRANTON, PENNSYLVANIA

To Verena Anderson

CHAPTER ONE

A shot echoed across the New Mexico desert. Not the zing of a rifle, but the loud quick report of a pistol. Jason Van Dyke urged the big stallion into a gallop and skirted the edge of the Gila River, racing up the bank. Tall brush and a sparse stand of cottonwood kept him from sight while his gaze combed the desert.

He flexed his left arm and winced. Two hours before, under cover of darkness, he'd crept too close to the camp of the gang of outlaws he'd been tracking and had caught a bullet in the shoulder. Next time he wouldn't come alone.

The relentless rays of the morning sun revealed the anger etched across his wind-browned face. He'd identified one of the men and a couple of maybes. At least now he knew who had raided the ranch, stolen fifty horses, and tried to kill his father. He'd get him, no matter how long it took. He glanced down at the tan linen shirt he wore. No fresh blood showed around the wide, dark stain.

The bleeding had stopped, but the bullet had to

be taken out. Tillie's cave, a day away, would be his only salvation. He smiled inwardly. Wouldn't do for the old judge to lose his only son to the gang he hated more than anybody else in California.

Jason wrinkled his forehead. Smoke and flames billowed from the desert. Forgetting his injured shoulder, he urged the stallion closer. Now he could see that flames enveloped what was left of a small, circled wagon train. He watched intently. No one moved near the wagons. The horses and mules were gone. His anger flared. The attackers must have murdered everyone.

The flames shot higher. Cautiously Jason backed his mount to a cottonwood tree. The fire had been set in the last few minutes. The men who had done it could still be close by.

Something moved from under a wagon. Jason reached for his rifle. The figure crawled several feet, then stood up and ran toward the river. Yellow hair glistened in the sunlight. Skirts swirled in a gust of wind. A woman.

He slapped the rump of the stallion and he leaped forward. If one of the gang saw her, they'd shoot her down like a jackrabbit running for cover.

Jason galloped straight for her. The woman angled away as if she were trying to escape. He swerved, galloping beside her. A rifle shot cracked. A bullet whizzed past them. He reached down, grabbed her around the waist, and carried the fighting, kicking female back to the river and into the cover of brush. "Let me go!" she screamed. Twisting, she sank white, even teeth into his upper arm.

He knocked her away with his chin. If he released her, she would run. If she ran up the river, they'd shoot her down. For several seconds he held her securely while she kicked at him furiously. "I won't hurt you," he said, exasperated. "I just saved your hide."

Suddenly she stopped fighting. He could smell the panic that engulfed her. She looked his way, her eyes wide with terror. "You're one of them. You killed Pa and all the others."

Jason eyed her swiftly. Her face was smudged with dust, and one braid of her golden hair had come undone. She appeared to be nineteen, maybe twenty. Blood covered one arm and the sleeve of the torn paisley dress she wore. Fine lace circled the high neck. It was not a dress that farm women wore. For some crazy reason he wanted to take care of her.

He flinched when he hoisted her behind him. Right now he could do without the pain in his shoulder. "I didn't kill anybody. If we don't get out of here, we'll both get blasted, and you're in the back, so you'll get it first." He felt her shudder as he urged the stallion into a gallop along the river's edge.

"Anybody else alive back there?" he asked.

"You got them all."

"Then hang on," he ordered. "If there's shooting, I'll have to swerve, and I don't intend to go back and pick you up if you fall."

She hung on.

Galloping wasn't helping his shoulder. A warm trickle of blood slid down his chest. He should stop, but now wasn't the time. He slowed the horse to a trot.

An hour later Jason pointed downriver and said, "We'll stop to rest the horse in that stand of cottonwood." He could almost hear the wheels in her mind as she plotted to get away from him, and he doubted he had the strength to run her down again.

"It's two days on horseback downriver to Fort Yuma," he warned. "More if you're on foot. And the desert? You wouldn't have a chance on foot in August with that sun eating you up."

She didn't answer.

At the stand of trees, she slid to the ground. He handed her the canteen. "Get some water," was all he said.

"Yes, sir," she snapped, and hurried the few steps to the river's edge.

He glanced across the river. Here the river narrowed to maybe thirty yards, and trees and high brush also protected the opposite side. For the past half hour, a lone Indian had been trailing them along the bank across the river. Rather unusual, unless the Indian knew Jason was wounded and meant to steal his guns and his horse.

When he moved to dismount, his mind turned foggy. He began to slide, slowly, inch by inch, to the ground. The fingers of his right hand still held the reins, and he centered his concentration on not letting go. If the stallion got away. . . . The thump on the ground jarred his shoulder, shooting pain down his arm. He tried to get up. Weakness overwhelmed him. He sank back to the damp edge of the river.

The girl cried out and ran to his side. He was aware of that through the blur of pain. "You're hurt. Why didn't you say so?"

She babbled on while she raised his head and gave him sips of cool water from the canteen, then carefully unbuttoned his shirt. "You must have been hit in the night. It's open again. How long have you been bleeding?" She didn't wait for an answer, nor did she seem to expect one.

He heard the rip of material, and figured she must be making a compress to stop the bleeding. "That bullet has to come out pretty soon. You know I could just leave you here and take your horse. You couldn't go after me."

He gathered strength to speak. "You'd better do it fast. There's an Indian across the river in the brush, and he's probably got a pony nearby. Ever heard what braves do to pretty white girls?" He paused for breath. "You got a name? I should know who the Indian brave got."

"Indians!" She remembered the stories she'd heard on the wagon train, and her hands trembled. "It wasn't Indians who killed everybody and set our wagons on fire."

"No, it wasn't Indians. White men who wanted your supplies and horses. Your wagon master should have known that traveling with five or six wagons was dangerous. No small wagon train has made it through on this trail for half a year."

"We broke off from the main train a couple of days ago to head for San Diego. The man leading us said Indians seldom attacked wagon trains down here."

"If the Indians have guns, they do. Around here the bandits are more dangerous than the Indians."

Jason sensed her fear when she held the compress against his wound. "Name's Cassie. Give me your gun—I'll shoot that blamed Indian."

Jason couldn't keep his lips from curving in a weak smile. "He's probably a much better shot with an arrow than you are with a gun. Just leave him alone and act like you don't see him."

Cassie tied a wide strip of her petticoat expertly around his chest and over his shoulder to hold the compress in place. "You mean just sit here until he kills us?"

"He's just watching. He'll do nothing as long as you don't reach for the pistol in my holster. You're good at tying up gunshots. Had lots of practice?"

"My father was a doctor. Men in St. Louis get shot too."

"Your father among the dead on that wagon train?"

Cassie nodded but didn't speak. He noticed that tears filled her eyes. For a city girl, she had grit.

When she spoke at last, her voice quavered. "You can't ride until you rest or you'll bleed to death."

Jason knew she was right. He unbuckled his holster. "Slide it out from under me, but don't let the Indian see the gun close to your hand. Let the Indian be, but if anybody else comes down that river, kill him." He squinted up at her. "Can you do that?"

"If I have to."

Jason closed his eyes. If Cassie decided to grab his horse and run, he was powerless to stop her.

Cassie's glance flew from the helpless man on the ground to the big stallion. With a good horse and a gun, she could follow the river to Fort Yuma, where she could find someone to take her to San Diego to Uncle Henry. Would the Indian follow her?

She looked again at the man who had grabbed her and dragged her up on his horse. He looked young in spite of the smudges of dirt on his face and a week-old beard. Under thirty, she guessed, and not bad looking.

Cassie sighed. Her pa had never let a man die, good or bad, if he could help it. If she left this man without his horse, he would die. Reluctantly she tied the stallion to a spot nearby where coarse green grass grew beside the river. In the weeks since she'd left St. Louis, she had learned the importance of food and water for the stock.

She untied the pack behind the saddle and made a makeshift pillow for the stranger. Here she was taking care of him like one of her pa's patients, and she didn't even know his name. She watched him sleep.

Now and then a flash of color reminded her that the Indian still watched from across the narrow river. When would he attack? All she could actually see was the colorful band and his long black hair. She shivered in spite of the desert heat. Was he waiting for the man to die before he attacked?

Several times she checked under the compress on the man's shoulder. The bleeding had stopped completely. She studied the location of the sun and wished she had the pocket watch that her pa had always carried. It must be near noon. Daylight would last another eight or nine hours.

The lead had to be taken out of the man's shoulder, and she had neither the tools nor the ability to do it. They had to be on their way. Cassie awakened him by wiping his face with cool water. "The bleeding has stopped. Can you get on your horse?"

He opened his eyes and a half smile curved his lips. "I had better. It's several hours to Tillie's cave, but she'll fix me up."

Cassie brought the stallion and helped him mount, then handed him his gun and holster and a full canteen of water. "If I have to bury you, I should know your name."

He grinned. "Jason, and you won't have to bury me."

"Who's Tillie? Your woman in Fort Yuma?"

"Tillie is a prospector in the desert. She's got a cave and the only water for miles in any direction. Fort Yuma is too far."

Jason reached out his good arm and hoisted her up behind him, then turned the horse into the deadly midday heat of the New Mexico desert.

He headed north, away from the river. The deep desert sand pulled at the horse's hooves as it made its way slowly through the thorny low weeds that grew in the sand. Sun pounded their heads.

"Is this Tillie one of your bunch?"

"I'm not with any bunch—I'm alone. Tillie's sort of famous around here—she's a crusty old prospector and a dead shot with a rifle. She's got a claim up there, and good water. They say she knows how to take out a bullet without chopping a man to pieces."

They rode on. Two hours passed, then three. The heat intensified, and Jason felt Cassie lean against his back. Had she fallen asleep? When he turned to look at her, she awakened instantly and asked, "How far to this Tillie?"

Neither of them seemed eager to waste words. "Eight, maybe ten hours. Want some water?"

She shook her head. "I'm used to the heat. You drink it."

He had to give her credit. She knew the jarring and heat could get to him, and if fever set in, he'd probably need all the water he could get. Still, he urged her to drink. Heat emanated from the sand like great blasts from a furnace. Later he might not be so rational, and for some crazy reason he didn't want her to die in the desert. "Are you from St. Louis?"

She nodded again.

Why would a man with a beautiful daughter—and Cassie would be beautiful once the dirt was scrubbed off—subject her to the dangerous trip across the desert at this time of year? "You said your father was a doctor. Why did he want to come way out here? Was he in some kind of trouble?"

"He certainly was not! He was coming out here to see his brother. Uncle Henry told him he could have a good practice in San Diego."

Jason looked up at the sun, trying to judge the hour. His vision blurred. His shoulder ached and pain crept through his body. He closed his eyes. He had to hold out long enough to get to Tillie's, so Cassie wouldn't be left alone in the desert.

Cassie worried. Now the horse moved as slowly as a man's walk, and the weight of two people didn't help. If the stallion gave out, Jason couldn't walk, at least not far. She felt Jason sway forward and pulled him upright. "If you'll stop for a second, I want to walk."

"Why?" he growled.

"Because my seat is tired."

He stopped. She slid to the ground and walked beside him. He didn't look good. "What is your landmark?" she asked. "If you pass out, I don't want to get stranded out here in this sandpile."

He grinned down at her, but his eyes looked glazed. He lifted one arm and pointed. "That mountain. It looks like a . . . a tepee. Do you see it?"

"I see it."

"At the base is Tillie's cave. There's a spring, and rocks, a couple of green trees. . . ."

His voice tapered off. Cassie looked up at him, trying to decide whether the flush on his face was from the scorching sun or fever. She grabbed the horse's bridle and pulled it along. "Cassie?" he said.

She looked up at him. "Yes?"

"Keep the horse between yourself and over there." He motioned to his left. "That Indian is about a mile behind us."

Cassie's fingers tightened on the reins. She peeked back toward the Indian. "Why is he following us?"

"Probably because he knows I'm wounded. Maybe he's waiting for me to fall off my horse. If I do, Cassie, grab the horse and get out of here. Go to Tillie, you'll be safe there."

For a bandit, he was awfully protective. She wondered why but didn't ask.

"Did you hear what I said?"

"I heard you. Drink some water, your face is all red."

"Not unless you do."

Cassie took the canteen and tipped it against her mouth, only wetting her lips. She handed the canteen back to Jason and watched his throat move as he swallowed. Good. Water would help control the fever.

Hour after hour Cassie forged ahead, leading the stallion. The sun seemed barely to move in the sky. Jason rode silently, his eyes closed. Now and then he teetered and caught himself. He was drifting; all color had disappeared from his face.

She had to get him out of the heat. Gradually quickening her pace, she began to run through the intense late-afternoon sun, leading the horse behind her. The dusty smell of dried flora filled her nostrils, nearly choking her.

Perspiration ran down her back and chest. Hot wind dried it quickly. She hurried on, avoiding rocks and cactus the best she could. She had to get him to Tillie's claim while he could still sit his horse. Twice she stopped and urged Jason to drink. He no longer argued with her about the water.

The hill he had pointed out seemed no closer. The heat of the sand burned through her boots and she dreamed of submerging her feet in icy water. Behind them, closer now, the Indian followed. She ran on, not daring to stop to rest.

CHAPTER TWO

*J*ason slumped forward on the horse, caught himself, and grasped the saddle horn. Cassie breathed in mouthfuls of torrid air, trying to calm her rising alarm. If he fell now, he would die on the desert. She stopped to give him water. The canteen was empty. She swallowed the panic that threatened. She would not let this desert get them.

Only hours ago she'd battled bullets and flames. "Give me your gun, Papa," she had whispered, "I'll reload for you." He hadn't answered her. Blood ran from his neck, draining his life onto the still-warm sand. She had tried to wad his shirt against his neck to stop the bleeding, but even as she pressed against the ragged hole, she had known he was dead.

When the shooting had stopped, she heard horses approach. Cassie had jerked a shawl over her head and held her breath. A man had crawled under the wagon. He smelled of sweat and rotgut whiskey. Beside her, she heard him turn her father's pockets inside out. Gold coins clinkled and fell to the sand. "J-J-Joe," he yelled. "Th-th . . . this guy's got double eagles." That had been no stuttering Indian.

Now she glanced back at Jason. He sat slumped forward, hand still gripping the saddle horn. "Jason?"

He didn't answer.

Cassie hurried on. The desert wind burned her cracked lips. She touched them with her tongue. It didn't help. She was tired, so tired, and so hot. Hotter than when the fire that burned the wagons had threatened her. Heat waves shimmered before her eyes. A mirage of green bushes appeared on the desert, testing her sanity. How much longer could she last?

Jason moaned. His hand slipped from the saddle horn. He crumpled forward, threatening to fall. Cassie grabbed him. With all her strength, she righted him in the saddle. "Hang on," she cried. "You've got to hang on." He sat, precariously balanced, his head resting on the horse's mane.

Cassie led the horse toward the base of the mountain. It seemed closer. She began to run. The deep sand pulled at her boots. She stumbled, fell to the ground. Prickly desert growth scratched her face. She shoved it away, gasped for breath. The heat, the awful heat, seemed to pin her to the sand.

She looked back. The Indian came closer. Now he was running toward her. From somewhere, she gathered strength and scrambled to her feet. She struggled forward, leading the horse as fast as her heat-torn body would move. She glanced behind her. The Indian had dropped back.

The green bushes appeared again in the distance. Was she going mad? She brushed a hand across her eyes. The green bushes didn't go away. They were real! She'd found Tillie's claim. She'd found water!

With a spurt of new strength she ran toward it, pulling the horse behind her. Water trickled from between two rocks, and a small bucket under it caught the flow. She led the horse beside a big rock, grabbed the bucket, climbed up, and emptied the pail of water over Jason, drenching him.

He jerked awake, but for only a second. "Hang on, Jason, until we get up to the cave."

A shot whistled high over her head. Cassie stood her ground. Anyone who was a decent shot wouldn't miss at that distance unless it was on purpose. Cupping her hands around her mouth, Cassie yelled, "Tillie! Tillie!"

Silence. Then a faint echo of her own voice came back. She called again. "Tillie!"

A sturdy, square figure holding a rifle appeared on the rocks above. "You got my water, what more you want?"

Only the long gray hair flying in the wind told Cassie that the person who pointed the rifle was a woman. "We need help. Man shot. Fever. Indians!"

The thick, tall woman came down the rocks as if they were a wide staircase, springing from one to the other with surprising agility. "Who is he? I don't see any Indians."

Cassie looked back. The Indian was gone. But where? Would he creep up later and kill them all? "His name's Jason. He's got a bullet in the shoulder, and fever is setting in. He'd heard about you and thought you could help him."

The old lady, maybe sixty judging from her coppery, wrinkled face, didn't bother to introduce herself. She looked disgusted. "When will you young fools learn to duck when somebody's shooting? Bullet still in there?"

Cassie nodded. The woman took the reins and Cassie cupped her hands and drank from the spring.

Tillie reset the bucket under the spring and let the horse drink. "Looks like you weren't much help—you look as bad as he does." The woman led the horse carrying Jason around to a path up the rise. Cassie followed, glancing behind her with every step. Where was the Indian?

Tillie's place was more cave than shack. Beside the entrance, under a rocky overhang, a clay wall blocked the late afternoon sun, forming a kind of shaded porch. Rocks closed in the other side. Only the front remained open to the wind and sun.

Together they got Jason to the ground under the overhang and rolled him onto a coarse wool blanket. "You his woman?"

"No, he grabbed me running from a burning wagon train."

"Saw the smoke way off by the river. He one of the bandits?"

"Why else would he be there?"

Jason groaned and Tillie tossed Cassie a gray towel, which at one time in its life might have been white. "There's water in the bucket over there. Cool him off while I see how bad he's shot up."

Cassie sloshed water generously on Jason's face and arms while Tillie opened his shirt and examined the wound. Dried blood covered his chest, mingling with the dark hair. At least her compress had stemmed the bleeding.

Tillie removed the compress. "Bullet has to come out right now. Build up the fire."

Cassie quickly tossed dry cactus limbs into the well-blackened circle of rocks on Tillie's "porch."

When the fire blazed, Tillie shoved the blades of two knives into the flames. When one reddened with heat, she poured whisky over the wound. Jason yelped, then lay ominously still. Cassie sucked in her breath. Was he unconscious, or worse?

Tillie eyed her suspiciously. "Thought he wasn't your man."

"He's not. I don't even like him."

Carefully, Tillie probed for the bullet. Cassie winced when Jason groaned. Tillie removed the bullet and cauterized the wound; then Cassie mopped up the new bleeding the way her father had taught her. Her hand brushed the crisp dark hair on Jason's chest. Quickly, Cassie pressed a compress against the wound.

"Hey, you're pretty spunky for a city girl, didn't even flinch when blood squirted all over your hand."

"My father was a doctor." She didn't elaborate. Her father had been a good doctor. He wanted to help people; that was his life. The fact that he paid little attention to his daughter hadn't been his fault. He had never gotten over the death of his wife. Cassie helped him and loved him. He had been all she had.

When Jason's bleeding was under control, Cassie applied a fresh compress and tied a wide band around his chest to hold the dressing in place.

Tillie stood, hands on hips, looking down at Jason. She wore coarse wool pants and a man's calico shirt. Even her rough leather boots smacked of masculine attire.

"He's too weak to be moved. He's a mess, must have been on the trail for a spell. Hand me that blanket. I'll get his clothes off and you can clean him up."

Cassie sat on the hard earth floor while Tillie removed Jason's clothes. She marveled at the rough old woman's gentleness as she slipped his arms from his shirt. She tossed Cassie his shirt, then his boots and pants.

Cassie started to roll them into a bundle when the jingle of coins caught her attention. She plunged her hand into a pants pocket and pulled out a handful of coins. Double eagles! Jason *was* one of the bandits!

Wordlessly, she returned the coins to his pocket. She'd have to be doubly careful, now that she knew he was one of them.

She reached for a small, clean cloth and wiped the blood off his stomach and arm. After rinsing the cloth in the bucket, she rubbed at the caked blood on his left hand. It was a callused hand, but the fingernails were neatly trimmed. He didn't fit her picture of a bandit. The boots were too new, and his trousers, though covered with dirt, were of fine, soft wool.

Jason stirred and asked for water. Cassie slid her arm under his head and held the cup to his cracked lips. He hadn't fared well in the sun, but then, neither had she. At least he had worn a hat. Her face was tight and dry and her forehead smarted. She ran her hand across it and winced.

Tillie handed her a jar. "Put some grease on it or by morning you'll be blistered. Should have worn a hat."

"I didn't exactly have time to look for a sunbonnet."

The foul-smelling grease helped, and Cassie spread some across Jason's face and the bridge of his nose. She noticed that he had a nice nose. After she finished, she leaned back against the coolness of the clay wall. Her eyes drooped closed. Exhaustion and hunger fought for first place in her misery.

How had she gotten herself into this awful situation? And how would she escape?

She had been eager to leave St. Louis when Papa got the letter from his brother in San Diego saying he needed a doctor on his ranch. She had hoped that leaving St. Louis might lighten her father's grief. Uncle Henry had described his fine house and promised they could live there.

Papa had believed the trip would be easy because the trail to San Diego had been broken by hundreds of immigrants. He bought passage for Cassie and himself on the wagon of a man who was traveling alone. The old fellow had seemed glad for company and someone to spell him at the reins.

Now Uncle Henry and his ranch seemed far away. Cassie had no money to buy passage on a wagon train from Fort Yuma, so, bandit or not, Jason was her only means of getting to San Diego, and she had better make certain he stayed alive.

The delightful aroma of sizzling salt pork reminded her acutely of her empty stomach. She opened her eyes to see Tillie dropping chunks of salt pork into a black frying pan over the fire. "You're skinny as a post," Tillie said. "When did you have your last meal?"

Cassie smiled. "Yesterday, I think." She rose unsteadily to her feet and lifted the bucket. "I'll get fresh water and clean up a little."

Tillie motioned to a ledge in the cave. "There's a piece of soap up there. You could do with a scrubbing."

Tillie dumped soaked beans in with the pork and Cassie's stomach growled in anticipation. How could beans and sowbelly smell like a banquet?

The heavenly smell of cooking food followed her down to the spring, or maybe she carried the delicious aroma with her. The late afternoon sun heated her back, and the cool spring water felt good when it ran over her head as she rubbed soap into her hair.

On a rock beside the spring she sat down to let her hair dry. Running her fingers through the long strands, she bent forward to let it catch the desert breeze. When she raised her head, she gasped in alarm. Not ten feet away, an Indian stood watching her. She jumped and backed against the tall rocks, glancing about frantically for a place to run.

The Indian was young, no more than fifteen, and dressed in rough wool pants and a too-big Army shirt open down the front. All the buttons were missing. Long black hair covered his proud head and was held in place with a turquoise-and-red band, the same colorful band she had glimpsed by the river.

Fear crawled up her spine, but she dared not acknowledge her terror. She stood up and eyed him belligerently. The only Indians she had encountered in St. Louis had been dirty and old. But the immigrants on the wagon train had told her chilling tales of Indian attacks. "Why are you following us?" she asked. "What do you want?"

The Indian didn't flinch at her brusque question, but neither did he come closer. "Food," he said.

Did he understand her words, or just the anger in her voice? No weapon appeared in his hand, although he was bound to be carrying a knife someplace on him. "Tillie has no extra food, especially not for Indians."

He stepped toward her threateningly. He must be understanding at least some of her words. Cassie looked quickly toward the cave. The Indian stood between her and the rock steps that led up. The only place she could run would be the open desert, and he would outpace her in seconds. She considered screaming for Tillie, but the Indian could have a knife in her chest before Tillie could reach for her rifle.

Her mind raced. He was only a boy, but taller than her five feet four inches, and his open shirt displayed a well-muscled chest. She had no means to overpower him; she would have to outsmart him, if she could make him understand. "If Tillie doesn't have enough food, I'll share my portion with you, but you'll have to let me go up to the cave to get it. It won't be ready for a while—you'll have to wait."

"Wait," he said.

Cassie scrambled up the rocks to the cave. Her panic exploded the minute she reached safety. "Indian! There's an Indian by the spring. He wants food!"

Jason raised his head and struggled to sit up. "Where?" he gasped.

Tillie glared at Jason. "Get back down." Then she told Cassie, "If there is an Indian by the spring and he planned to harm you, you would be dead by now. How do you know he wants food?"

Bewildered at Tillie's lack of fear, Cassie tried to suppress her own alarm. "Because he told me."

Tillie shrugged. "They pick up a word here and there. Is there only one man?"

"He's not a man, he's a boy, maybe fifteen." Cassie shook her head in disbelief. "Aren't you afraid of Indians?"

Tillie stirred the beans in the big pot. "I have no quarrel with them. They drink from my spring. I leave them alone."

Minutes passed. Cassie's apprehension returned. Would the Indian attack her when she brought food?

Jason moaned, and Cassie kneeled beside him and checked the compress over his wound. A spot of blood had soaked through the layers of cloth. "You could have hemorrhaged when you tried to get up and fight Indians. It's the brave we saw by the river. He's only a boy."

Jason didn't answer. Cassie checked the bandage. The bleeding had stopped. She leaned back against the clay wall, enjoying the heavenly aroma of cooking food, and thought about the Indian boy. Why had he followed them? Was he biding his time, waiting to kill them?

When the beans were tender, Tillie filled a tin bowl and handed it to Cassie. Cassie headed for the steps and Tillie stopped her. "Don't go down there. Set his food behind that rock, but you eat first. The Indian can wait."

Cassie shook her head. She wanted to be done with the Indian. "I don't want a hungry savage lurking around my plate," she insisted. Reluctantly she carried the plate the few steps to the big boulder. The Indian was nowhere to be seen.

CHAPTER THREE

*J*ason watched from where he lay on the blanket as Tillie handed Cassie a bowl of beans and settled herself on the rough wooden bench. Tillie frowned thoughtfully. "Wonder what an Indian brave is doing out here by himself." Concern flashed across Tillie's face. "Any rumors of an uprising along the trail? They could be scouting for water and a place to hide. Are you sure the boy is alone?"

Jason moved his shoulder and suppressed a groan from the effort.

Cassie frowned at Jason, then answered Tillie's question. "We met no one on the trail to tell us anything, not after the main part of the train headed north. It wasn't Indians who burned our wagons, it was white men. One of them stuttered, and he wore a paisley shirt. I'll never forget him."

Tillie checked her rifle, then moved it closer to the cave entrance. "We'll sleep light tonight."

"I'll be tending Jason if he needs anything. I'll wake you if I hear noises."

Tillie's wry grin displayed a missing front tooth.

"If Indians decide to take over this place, you won't hear them. And if the Indian boy is alone, he won't likely harm us after we've shared our food with him." She motioned toward the rock. "Get his dish. If he ate, we're probably safe, at least from him."

In seconds Cassie returned. "It's empty, and clean. He must have washed it in the spring."

Tillie nodded but said nothing.

Cassie scooped bean broth from the pot into a tin cup and sat down on the blanket beside Jason. "Can you take some broth?"

The corners of his lips turned up in a weak smile. "I wondered when you were going to ask."

She propped his head a little higher with an extra blanket and laid her palm on his forehead before spooning broth between his lips. The pain in his shoulder had relented a little and the broth eased his burning throat. He felt cooler, perhaps because the desert sun had dropped below the horizon.

He watched her intently while she fed him, and he noticed she reacted warily to his constant gaze. She was still afraid of him.

"Will you take me to San Diego?" she asked. "I have an uncle there."

"I'm not going that far. I plan to cross the desert to Fort Yuma, then go into the mountains. You won't be able to handle the desert heat, and once we pass Yuma, the way I'm going, there will be no wagon trains."

"I'm not afraid of the desert. I walked most of a day to get here. I told you I can handle heat."

"And if the one watering hole is dry, can you go another day, maybe more, without water? How about an Indian attack? Or perhaps running into the horse gang driving wild mustangs to Mexico? You wouldn't last an hour once those men spotted you. Besides that, you haven't got a horse."

"If you can get through, why can't I?"

"Because you're a woman." He closed his eyes. "I'll take you to Fort Yuma. You'll have to join a wagon train there. With all the settlers going west, you'll find a place."

He knew Cassie wanted to argue more, but how could he endanger her life by taking her with him into the mountains, where the gang that had tried to kill his father could be waiting to ambush him? Somebody wanted the judge's land and the abundance of water supplied by the underground spring that surfaced on his property, the only year-round water for miles in any direction.

Jason watched Cassie move gracefully around the cave. She washed the spoon and cup from the broth she had fed him, then sat cross-legged on the sandy floor, gazing out at the endless expanse of desert. She propped her elbow on one knee and cupped her chin with her hand. "Tillie, how long will it be before Jason can travel?"

"If he's got any sense, he'll wait a week."

Jason groaned inwardly. He couldn't wait a week; he had to get back to the ranch. The old judge might try something foolish, like coming to look for him. He closed his eyes.

He heard Cassie get to her feet and fill a cup with water, then felt her closeness when she lay down on the edge of the blanket beside him. "I'll stay with you in case you need anything in the night."

In the middle of the night Jason awoke, needing water. The silence of the cave prevailed, and the moon made a brilliant path across the mouth of the cave. His tongue felt parched and swollen, and the sweet taste of bean broth still remained. He raised his head to see where Cassie had left the cup of water, then reached for it.

The cool liquid tasted good trickling down his throat.

On the edge of his blanket, Cassie lay curled up and sleeping, but not peacefully. Tears slid from under her thick, dark lashes and onto her hand under her cheek. She moaned, and a tearing sob escaped. "Papa," she whispered.

He knew so little about her, only that she had grown up in St. Louis and had worked with her father. That had been obvious in the quick, experienced way she had stopped his bleeding. Her father must have been a good man; Cassie had inherited his caring. Back by the river, she could have taken Jason's horse and left him to die. He couldn't have stopped her.

Jason smiled slightly but his dry, cracked lips ended the smile. Cassie's head moved back and forth as if she were denying her dream, then she turned her face again in Jason's direction. Tears no longer fell. He wanted to reach out and brush aside the long golden hair that fell across her face, but he reserved his strength.

The moon dipped lower and lit a silvery path across her body. He'd never encountered a woman quite like her before. She was kind, spirited, and not afraid of every shadow—even sort of pretty. Too bad he had to put her on a wagon train in Yuma. He might never see her again.

The next two days passed in a blaze of heat, and Jason's temperature rose, making him incoherent part of the time. Cassie bathed him constantly with cool water from the spring. She knew nothing else to do.

Tillie cooked jerky and more beans and helped Cassie wring out wet towels to lay on Jason's head and chest. "The Indian boy is still around. I can't figure out why. When I put out food, he eats it and washes the empty bowl."

"Do you think he's waiting for . . . for. . . ." Cassie couldn't say the word. She must keep Jason alive. She stared at the empty water bucket, then at the setting sun. They needed water to last through the night. Even the small pail that held drinking water was empty. Twice when she'd hurried down to the spring in the middle of the day to fill the bucket, the Indian boy had been nowhere around.

Now it was nearly dark. She had to bring in water for the night. She took the largest wooden bucket and headed for the spring below.

"Be careful," Tillie said softly.

Cassie paused at the edge of the porch uncertainly. The sinking sun made long scary shadows of the big rocks, and the spring looked a mile away. Step by step she descended the rocks, slowly, as if each step could be her last. For the first time she realized the desert had sounds at night. Sounds like running feet, or lizards scurrying from rock to crevice.

Twilight closed in. Each pebble that moved frightened her. Where was the Indian now?

At the spring, Jason's tethered horse nibbled at the coarse grass. At least the Indian hadn't stolen the stallion. Why did she jump back when it moved? She knew it was there.

She set the bucket under the spring and waited nervously for it to fill. It seemed to take forever. She waited. They needed a full bucket of water to get Jason through the night.

When it was full, she started carefully up the rocks, one step at a time.

She heard no sound until a soft voice broke the silence. "The water is heavy. I'll carry it up for you."

Cassie whirled, nearly dropping the bucket. The young Indian stood in the waning light, reaching his hand toward the pail.

Cassie jumped back, nearly losing her balance.

She glanced at the rocks below. A scream gurgled in her throat, then died there. "You—you speak English." The desert wind caught his buttonless shirt and flapped it around him. Her knees buckled, and she sat down on a rock.

"I won't hurt you. My name is Felipe. You have given me food, and I am grateful. I'll carry the water for you."

"How did you learn to speak English like that?"

His face hardened in the last rays of the twilight. "From an Englishman who hated Indians."

Cassie stared at him in disbelief. Somehow the fact that he could speak English made him less frightening. He picked up the bucket and headed up the steps. "Come, the old lady will worry if you are gone too long."

He stepped aside for Cassie to go up the rocks ahead of him. With each step, she watched him warily. At the top of the rocks he set the bucket down. "Thank—" she began, but he was gone.

Cassie lifted the bucket into the cave. "The Indian. He's out there. I talked to him."

Tillie grabbed her rifle.

"No. Don't shoot at him. He won't hurt us. He speaks English just like we do."

Still holding her rifle, Tillie gazed into the darkness. "Don't think that because he speaks English he won't kill us in our sleep."

"He won't, I know he won't. He carried the water for me. He could have killed me tonight. I didn't even hear him until he spoke. His name is Felipe. Put the gun away. He won't hurt us."

Tillie set the rifle aside. "So now you're an authority on Indians." She motioned in Jason's direction. "Better take care of your partner there. He needs water." Her tone was brusque, but not angry.

Cassie slid her arm under Jason's head and urged sips of water between his lips, then sponged him with cool water. She lowered her cheek to his forehead. "He seems cooler."

"It's about time. Funny how taking care of a man makes you fond of him." She gazed into the distance. "I remember an old fellow who came to me. All shot up, he was. I nursed him back to health and wouldn't have been at all disappointed if he had stayed for a spell." She grinned. "He still stops by now and then to bring me supplies."

Cassie bristled and didn't know why. "I'm trying to get Jason well so he can take me to San Diego." Was that the reason ripples of excitement washed over her whenever she was near him? Then she added, "I have no money to buy a space on a wagon train. How else can I get there?"

The next day the sun blazed high in the sky. It was around noon, Cassie figured, when the Indian boy moved like lightning into the cave. Tillie grabbed her rifle.

"No!" Cassie cried. "Don't shoot. It's Felipe."

"Many riders are coming," Felipe said.

Tillie stared at Felipe, then lowered her rifle. "You're just a kid. What you doing here?"

Felipe pointed into the desert. Only waves of heat shimmered on the horizon. "There."

Far across the desert, an almost imperceptible cloud of dust rose skyward. Tillie glanced toward Jason, who was struggling to sit up. "You, Indian, stay with him. Don't let him make a sound."

Tillie checked her rifle and placed a supply of ammunition beside it. "Cassie, hand me that gun, then get the horse around back."

"I've hidden the stallion in a cave," Felipe said. "No one will see him."

"Good," Tillie whispered.

Cassie picked up the other rifle. "I don't know how to shoot this thing. Got a pistol? I can shoot a pistol."

The dust became horses and riders. Tillie backed out of view and motioned Cassie to do the same. "A pistol won't carry far enough. I'll show you how to load a rifle. Even if you can't hit anything, you can scare them. Don't fire unless I tell you. At the rate they're moving, they haven't been long on the trail. They may just want water."

Cassie lay prone on the sandy floor of the ledge, watching the riders advance. Fear scudded up her spine. She could tell Tillie was scared too, by her quick movements and the crisp orders she gave.

Felipe crept up beside Cassie. "Where are the man's pistols? You may need them. I'll load them for you."

She hadn't even thought about the time it took to reload. She pointed to a wooden box against the far wall. "In there. Cartridges in the gunbelt."

The riders came closer. Felipe returned, crawling along the floor, and laid Jason's two guns beside her. He began shoving cartridges into place.

"They're leading two saddled horses with no riders," Tillie said in a hoarse whisper. "They've left two dead men behind." One of the men galloped ahead of the others. "I count eight men."

The head man approached the well, and the others joined him. They gazed into the rocks, one for an unusually long time. Cassie kept her head down. "Maybe they don't know you're here," she said softly.

"Everybody who uses the trail knows I'm here. Could be they're looking for your man. Is he one of them?"

"I don't know." Suddenly Cassie felt very protective of Jason. "Even if he is, we can't let them take him. He'd die on the trail."

One at a time, the men watered their horses. Time seemed suspended in the hot, dry air. They talked among themselves, splashing water on their faces, filling canteens. One took off his hat and poured water over his head. A jagged white scar on his cheek stood out against his tanned skin— and he wore a paisley shirt!

Cassie lay silently, afraid to breathe. If they came

after Jason. . . . Perspiration ran down her face and tasted salty on her lips.

She heard the click of a pistol being cocked. A man, gun in hand, started up the steps to the cave.

CHAPTER FOUR

*J*ason tried again to sit up. His vision blurred. He lay back down, listening, watching. "One man is coming up," the Indian boy whispered.

Weakly Jason nudged himself a couple of yards along the sandy floor of the cave. If it was one of the bandits, Cassie wouldn't have a chance. He'd figure she was the escaping woman they'd shot at and missed. He'd never let her live to identify them.

With strength from somewhere, Jason grabbed Cassie's ankle securely with his good hand. She tried to kick free of his grasp but he held on. "Get back," she whispered. "I think it's the men who burned the wagons."

He pulled her his way and shoved her behind him. The back of the cave was dark. He pushed her against the rock wall and shielded her with his body. "Stay down. They won't let a witness live."

He motioned to the Indian for a pistol. Felipe handed him one, then took up the rifle next to Tillie.

A coarse voice called out from below: "Old

woman, any strangers up there? Anybody stop for water?"

Tillie didn't lower her rifle. "Not a soul. Looking for somebody?" Jason marveled at the composure in Tillie's voice.

The voice hesitated. "A woman . . . and a man on a brown stallion."

"Ain't seen no white folks for a couple of weeks."

Jason heard Tillie slowly let out her breath. The man must have changed his mind about coming up.

Cassie laid her cheek against the sandy floor. Jason felt her shudder.

"They're leaving," Felipe whispered.

Cassie crawled to the mouth of the cave and watched the bandits straggle into the desert. She watched until all she could see was a blur of horses' rumps and backs of men, but in her mind she still envisioned the man with the paisley shirt coming up the stone steps. Satisfied that the bandits were gone, she turned on Jason. "I recognized the clothes on the man coming up the steps. He was one of the bandits that burned our wagons, I know he was."

Jason lay on his back now, eyes closed. "And they know that a woman escaped from the train. Somebody took a shot at you when you ran from the burning wagons."

Cassie didn't answer right away, and by the time she had recalled the rifle shot in the flurry of Jason grabbing her from the desert, he was asleep.

Tillie got to her feet and propped her rifle against the rocky wall. She grinned at Felipe. "Where did you hide the stallion? You probably saved our skins."

Felipe glowed. "In a cave I discovered yesterday. I'll get him out."

"Better leave him there for a spell. They could come back. Bandits, that's what they were. Probably going to Fort Yuma to celebrate."

When Felipe stood up to leave, Tillie called him back. "Food will be ready before long. I'll call out when it's ready."

The next morning Jason opened his eyes and asked for breakfast. The fever was gone.

Cassie added fuel to the hot coals and hurried to make biscuits and warm beans. "What's the big hurry?" Tillie asked. "He hasn't starved to death yet, and I don't reckon he will in the next hour." Tillie's tone was serious, but laced with humor.

"The quicker he regains his strength, the sooner I'll get to San Diego."

Jason felt good. Soon he'd be able to travel. He watched Cassie prepare breakfast and smiled to himself. She looked like a kid, with those two braids hanging down her back.

When Cassie brought his food, she acted nervous, unsure of herself. One minute she was fighting bandits with the courage of a pioneer woman, and the next she was a young girl, uneasy around a man. "Would you like me to feed you?" she asked.

"I'd like you to sit beside me and tell me what I've missed. How long was I out of it?"

"We've been here for four days."

He spooned beans into his mouth, then bit into a hot biscuit and nodded. "Where's the Indian kid?"

"You mean the dangerous Indian brave you said was following me? The one you tried to get up and fight the night we arrived?"

Jason smiled. "Looks like you tamed him."

"He didn't need taming. He's as civilized as we are. Right now, he's building better steps down to the spring."

Felipe stepped onto the ledge and Cassie called out to him. "Come and meet Jason. Yesterday he was groggy."

Felipe came slowly into the cave. "Are you well? I believe the men who burned the wagons were the ones who stopped to get water. We should have shot them."

Jason's anger colored his words. "You can't kill a man without a trial."

Felipe shrugged. "White men do it. You are not a judge."

"My father is. You, Felipe, have a lot to learn."

"Learning is not good. It makes a man strange to his own people."

Jason motioned Felipe to sit down. "Is that why you left your tribe?"

"My tribe is at the Valley of the Springs near San

Diego. They sent me into the desert to become an acceptable warrior."

Jason looked long and hard at Felipe; then his eyes softened. "And did you learn to be a warrior?"

Felipe lowered his gaze. "I wandered alone on the desert for many days. A band of kindly Indians found me and took me to their chief. He taught me to be a warrior. He taught me that not all white men are bad and not all Indians are good."

Jason smiled. "You learned an important lesson. You learned to think for yourself."

Cassie nodded. "He hid your horse when the men approached. Perhaps he saved our lives. It doesn't matter to me that he's an Indian, he's our friend."

Jason's face reflected agreement.

Tillie stood at the entrance to the cave. "Indian or not, there's water to be fetched and fuel to be gathered."

Felipe picked up the water bucket. "I'll get water and fuel for the fire."

Tillie turned to Jason. "Can you sit up?"

Jason raised himself on one elbow and struggled to sit up. Cassie slipped an arm under his shoulders to help him. She tried to shake off the warmth that flooded through her when he gripped her arm and pulled himself to a sitting position. He teetered and she steadied him. His muscles rippled under her hand.

"Stay with him, Cassie, so he doesn't tip over.

He doesn't need his head banged on the ground," Tillie said.

Cassie sat beside him, watching him carefully. "In that bunch of men who came to the spring yesterday, one had a jagged scar on his cheek."

"Did they see you?"

"I don't think so. You pulled me out of sight, remember? They led two saddled horses without riders."

Jason tried to remember the face of the man who had shot him close to the bandits' camp. He'd had a scar, Jason was almost certain.

Beads of perspiration formed on his forehead, and Cassie ordered him to lie down. "You can sit up again in about an hour."

Tillie sat on her bench cleaning a rifle. "I'll teach you to shoot this rifle, Cassie, soon as I get it cleaned. If you plan to live in the West, you'd better know how to shoot quick and straight. How's your aim with a pistol?"

"Fair. My father taught me some before we left St. Louis."

"You have to be better than fair."

Felipe stacked fuel for the fire next to the blackened circle of rocks that was Tillie's stove. Tillie looked his way. Cassie suspected Tillie was becoming rather fond of the young Indian. "How about you, Felipe—know how to shoot a rifle?"

He grimaced. "I was taught in San Diego by an expert, but I haven't practiced in the three years since."

"Tomorrow morning, early, we'll do a little shooting." Tillie loaded the rifle she held. "I'll teach you two to down a man at fifty yards." She raised the rifle. "See that rock with the pebble on top?"

Tillie pulled the trigger. The pebble jumped into the air. Cassie gasped. Felipe smiled.

Cassie glanced at Jason, who was struggling to sit up again. She hurried to help him.

Seconds later, Tillie set her rifle aside and hurried to the steps. "Old Charlie's coming with supplies."

Cassie joined Felipe at the cave entrance and watched Tillie make her way down the rocks. She got to the spring before Charlie. "That must be the friend she talked about," Cassie said, but didn't elaborate. It was obvious Tillie was glad to see him. Charlie wore a battered felt hat that shaded his desert-browned face, but his spry step belied the lined skin.

Tillie tethered his mule beside the spring and helped unload its pack. When she mounted the stone steps with Charlie, Tillie's face glowed.

The old prospector seemed surprised to find Jason and Cassie there. "Hope you folks ain't aiming to go beyond the fort," he said.

"I'm going west to the mountains," Jason said. "I plan to put Cassie on a wagon train at Fort Yuma. She has an uncle in San Diego."

The old man wiped his face with a red handkerchief. "No wagons leaving the fort. Too dangerous.

Bandits been robbing and burning the wagons." He motioned toward Felipe. "The Indian boy going with you?"

"Maybe so."

"Don't let the settlers see him. They think it's Indians who been robbing the trains. They'll shoot him on sight."

Jason frowned. Now what would he do with Cassie? At best, Fort Yuma was a rowdy place. With a bunch of unhappy settlers wanting to leave, it would be wild. How could he leave Cassie there alone to wait until the wagons could leave?

The old man joined Tillie to help her unpack the supplies he had brought. Cassie went to sit on the blanket beside Jason. "Now will you take me to San Diego? I won't stay in Fort Yuma until the wagons decide to make a run for it. I've seen what those bandits do."

"We have only one horse. Do you plan to walk across the desert?"

"If I have to."

"And carry provisions and water for days? That's a desert out there, with killing heat and very little water."

"I saw Papa's map on the train. There's water at C . . . C . . . some creek, and again at a place called Keystone."

"Corrizo Creek," Jason supplied. "It could be dry. Have you any idea how many days it will take to walk to Keystone?"

Cassie jumped to her feet. "Felipe will go with me. We'll get there, with or without your help."

Jason shook his head in dismay. He had planned to go straight west from Corrizo Creek to his home in the mountains east of San Diego, but he couldn't risk the danger of taking Cassie that way. The trail he had planned to take was known as Killers' Row, a place where every bandit on the desert camped. With Cassie he would have to follow the wagon trail to Temecula, and that would add days to the trip. Felipe could be a big help on the trail, if Jason could keep the settlers from shooting him.

Jason lay back down on the blanket and closed his eyes. He had to gain back his strength before he could go anyplace. There was a small Mexican camp a half day off the trail. They would sell him horses if they had any.

He looked toward Cassie. "I'll take you on the immigrant trail as far as San Luis Rey. That's two days northeast of San Diego. You and Felipe can make it from there; it's high desert and cooler."

Cassie beamed. "We'll be ready. Tillie is teaching me to shoot the rifle. I won't be a burden, I promise."

For Jason, the next days passed quickly. The fever had sapped his strength, but each day his body strengthened. From the porch of the cave, he watched Cassie perfect her aim with the rifle. He had to smile at her determination.

On the third day he made his way down the steps

to stand beside her. "Not bad. You're becoming quite a shot. How about you, Felipe? We may need all the rifle power we can get."

Cassie handed the rifle to Felipe. He aimed and splattered a rock at fifty yards. Jason grinned. "We won't waste ammunition teaching you."

When Jason was able to walk farther, they took short hikes into the desert in the cool of the night. "Stay with him, Cassie, so he doesn't overdo," Tillie ordered. "I don't intend to help drag him back if he drops out there."

Jason liked walking in the desert with Cassie beside him. One night they walked farther than usual from Tillie's cave, and he pulled her against his chest and kissed her. He didn't know why he did it, and the sudden exhilaration that passed over him unnerved him.

Cassie stepped away. "What was that for?"

He smiled at her uncertainly. "For saving my life. Is that the first time you've been kissed for saving somebody's life?"

Cassie kicked at the sand nervously. "I've never saved anyone's life before."

Jason waited three more days until he felt he had regained sufficient strength to make the long trip. He worried about his father and the men who had tried to kill him. Would they return to finish the job? "We'll leave tomorrow morning at first light—get as many hours on the trail as possible before the heat sets in."

Preparation for the trip took little time. Tillie

packed a small portion of flour and jerked beef. "Don't like you leaving with no more than two days' food along. You sure you can find that camp?"

"I'll find it," Jason assured her. "If we load down the horse with supplies, we'll lose him in the heat. We'll carry all the water we can."

The next morning, a pink sky in the east promised a scorching day. Tillie jammed a battered straw hat on Cassie's head. Cassie bade Tillie goodbye and started down the steps behind Felipe and Jason. Suddenly Cassie turned and ran to Tillie and hugged her tightly. "Thank you," she said, and scampered back down to where Felipe and Jason waited with the horse.

Cassie brushed a hand across her eyes, and she sensed Jason's gaze, although he didn't speak. So she would miss Tillie; it was none of his business if she felt a little teary saying good-bye.

Leading the stallion, they made their way west along the rocky desert floor. Heat beat on their shoulders and parched their lips. As the sun ascended, only an occasional sip from a canteen gave them relief. By noon, she knew why Jason had said she couldn't make it alone.

No one spoke. Felipe walked beside them, his shoulders straight, head high. He wore an old felt hat that Charlie had pulled from his pack. Waves of heat rippled up from the sand, baking Cassie's feet and legs; hot wind scorched her face. No wagon wheels cut a trail, only occasional horse or mule tracks, but Jason seemed to know the way.

The sun dipped behind the mountains to the west and Jason insisted they stop for the night. He could see Cassie was exhausted, and the heat had nearly brought him down. He knew Cassie was tired and hungry but he forbade her to use water to make biscuits. She didn't argue. The jerked beef did little to fill their stomachs.

"Tomorrow morning we leave the trail and go south to find the Mexican camp," Jason said. "We'll need two more horses and a good amount of supplies."

"How will we find this trail again?" Cassie asked.

"We'll find it."

Felipe had said little, but now he spoke. "I know of no Mexican village."

"It's a camp. I was there three weeks ago."

"A camp could be gone by now."

"Don't even think that way," Jason said. "We must have horses and supplies."

The next morning Jason tried to brush aside the strange uneasiness that assailed him when they left the trail and headed south. Could the Mexican camp he had watered at as he tracked the bandits have been only a temporary camp? Felipe evidently had been this way before. Jason felt groggy. He shook his head to clear it. He was leading them into a vast expanse of desert with no trail. Had he turned off at the right place, or had the fever impaired his sense of direction? They could wander forever in this arid pile of rocks and sand.

Three hours, passed, then four. The September heat resembled the oven of a stove stoked full of coal. The horse stumbled along behind Felipe, who held the lead. Hot, ankle-deep sand tugged at their feet.

They pushed on for another hour. Suddenly Jason stopped. Relief surged over him, clogging his throat. For the first time in his life, he'd been scared: not for himself, but for Cassie. He swallowed and pointed. "There it is."

In the distance, a small shack and two trees broke the ocean of sand. He saw tears form in Cassie's eyes. She blinked them away.

As they approached the oasis, the shack became two shacks, one with its side collapsed. Several men walked slowly around the area. He looked more closely. Each appeared to carry a rifle on his shoulder.

Jason jerked them to a quick stop. "The camp has been taken over." He crouched in the sand and motioned Cassie and Felipe to do the same. "I'll go in alone."

"I'll go with you," Cassie whispered.

"No," he ordered. "There's no way I can protect you if those men decide they want a little female company. Remember the men who stopped at Tillie's? It could be them. Stay back until I signal it's safe."

"We'll wait," she said.

Jason led his thirsty horse directly to the spring and waited while he drank his fill. Cassie motioned Felipe to stay back and crawled along the hot sand for a closer look. She held her gun clear of the sand. If Jason needed help, she wanted it handy.

She kept her eyes on Jason's tall figure walking slowly toward the shack. A man came out, pointing a gun at Jason's chest. Jason didn't budge.

Cassie tensed, fear streaking through her. Then she watched in bewilderment as the man holstered his gun and reached out and shook Jason's hand. Her breath swished out like an exploded balloon.

She was about to jump to her feet and go forward to join Jason when the man turned, shaded his eyes, and looked in her direction. It was the man in the paisley shirt.

CHAPTER FIVE

*J*ason's nerves threatened to explode as he dickered for two worn horses and supplies for the trip. He'd introduced himself as an immigrant from Tucson headed for Los Angeles. He was certain these men were the bandits who had raided his ranch and threatened to kill his father. He could do nothing about them now, but he catalogued each face in his mind.

He forced himself not to glance in the direction where Cassie and Felipe waited. If the bandits were also the ones who had burned Cassie's wagon train, one glimpse of the woman and he would be a dead man.

Jason divided the flour and jerky he had purchased and secured them to the backs of the two thin horses. He forced himself to work slowly, as if he were in no hurry to be out of the camp.

"Here he comes," Cassie muttered, and began to get up.

Felipe pushed her back down on the sand. "He

50

knows where we are. Let him get clear of the camp."

Cassie's mind whirled with questions. Were the men in the camp his friends, or had he bluffed his way through to get horses and supplies?

When Jason came within a few yards, Felipe jumped to his feet and ran to meet him. Cassie stood up and waited. Jason's smile turned her qualms to thudding heartbeats. "We have horses, and enough supplies to take us to Keystone. Let's get out of here."

He hooked a coiled rope over the saddle horn and motioned Cassie to his horse. "We'll ride for a while."

Cassie reached for the back hem of her skirt and pulled it up, diaper fashion, and mounted. The front of the skirt gave her legs a measure of protection from the searing sun. Felipe and Jason mounted the other two horses and Jason led them at a brisk trot back in the direction of the trail they had left that morning.

"We should reach the Colorado River by nightfall," he said, "and tomorrow pick up the main Gila Trail on the other side."

Cassie rode beside Jason. What a relief not to walk in the burning sand. "The men at the camp were the ones who stopped at Tillie's cave," she said. "I remember the paisley shirt one of them wore. Why are they staying in the desert so long?"

"I don't know. Maybe they like the heat."

His answer angered Cassie, but she said no more.

Why waste her breath in the relentless heat? He didn't intend to tell her anything. She shrugged. What did it matter? He would leave them at San Luis Rey and she would never see him again. Why did that make her sad?

By the time the sun dipped behind the mountains in the west, her eyes burned from searching the endless expanse of sand and low brush for the river.

"There it is!" Felipe yelled, and galloped ahead.

Cassie and Jason followed. At the river, Cassie's breath caught in her throat. It had to be at least a hundred yards to the other side, and muddy water swirled and twisted in the fast-moving current. "We can't cross here!" she cried.

At the bank, Jason lifted her to the ground, and the touch of his hands on her waist made her want him to kiss her again, the way he had kissed her near Tillie's place. But he didn't. He just surveyed the river thoughtfully.

"We have to cross here," he said. "There should be a sandbar for footing." He led the horses to drink, then gave each a portion of oats. "We'll cross in the morning."

"Will there be Indians after we cross? I've heard they live along the river."

"If we run into any, they probably won't bother us. They don't like guns. And the only thing we have that they might value would be my stallion."

Heat still hung in the air, and Jason worried more about Cassie than Indians. Would she be able to withstand the grueling temperatures of the next two days? At Corrizo, an underground spring surfaced, but in September it could be dry.

Now he watched Cassie scoop water from the river with her hands, wetting her face and arms and splashing more on her neck. Water dripped from her hair, causing it to curl around her face. She cupped her hands and drank from the river.

Under a tree at the river's edge, Felipe built a circle of rocks for a fire and piled dry sticks and brush in the pit. The fire blazed, adding to the heat.

Cassie made biscuits from the flour Tillie had sent along, and Jason boiled coffee in a kettle. They ate biscuits and jerky washed down with big mouthfuls of fragrant coffee. For the first time in two days, hunger ceased to gnaw at Jason's stomach. He knew Cassie and Felipe had suffered the same hunger, but not once had either of them complained.

Darkness came, and they sat around the campfire enjoying the slight respite from the heat. "Felipe, will you go back to your people when we get to San Diego?" Cassie asked.

He didn't answer right away, but when he did, anger colored his voice. "Do you mean to the Indians? They laugh at me when I tell them that they should learn the white man's language, that they could bargain better and wouldn't always be cheated." He sighed. "But they're too stubborn to learn."

Cassie wrinkled her forehead, perplexed. "But you learned."

"I had no choice. When I was a baby, my father—the chief—sold me to an Englishman for four bags of corn."

"But why, Felipe? Didn't your father love you?"

"The rains did not come. His people were hungry."

Cassie's heart went out to Felipe. How rejected he must feel. "The Englishman, why did he want an Indian baby?"

"So his wife would not die of sorrow over the death of their child." Felipe looked into the distance as if he were remembering. "His wife was a beautiful, loving Spanish señora. She raised me as if I were her own."

No one interrupted Felipe's story, and he went on. "But her husband, the Englishman, who came here and made himself rich, thought it a challenge to teach a 'stupid' Indian to speak in the same manner that he spoke." Felipe sighed. "I grew up as a white boy, but the proud Englishman could not change the color of my skin."

"Do your adopted parents live in San Diego?"

"The beautiful señora who was my mother died, and the proud Englishman took his wealth and returned to England. That was three years ago."

"He just left you to fend for yourself?"

"He packed my clothes in his fine carriage and delivered me back to my Indian father."

Tears burned in Cassie's eyes, tears for the loneliness and hurt that echoed in Felipe's voice. "And what did your father say?"

"I do not know. I couldn't understand his language."

"Oh, Felipe, how awful!"

"I understand it now. I have learned to be a warrior and not to kill for the sake of killing."

For the first time, Jason entered the conversation. "If you find the need, you'll be welcome at my ranch near San Luis Rey. I run beef."

"I will decide for myself where I'll live and what I'll do."

Jason grinned. "You do that, but don't lose track of us."

Cassie got to her feet and tossed a few twigs on the fire, and then, with Felipe's help, stored their supplies safely for the night.

When that was finished, she walked to the river's edge and gazed into the swirling water. The full skirt of her dark cotton dress hung limp and tattered from the many washings it had received at Tillie's spring. Now dust from the desert had turned it a pasty brown. Unbraiding her hair, she raised it off her neck in search of a cooling breeze. In the darkness a white moon bathed the sand in silver.

"Your hair is beautiful," Jason said, behind her.

"It's thick and hot, and I wish I could take a bath."

"You can, if you don't mind being looped to the end of a rope."

Refusal was on her lips, but the cool water looked heavenly. "I can't take off my clothes."

"You'll get cold sleeping in wet clothes. We'll find a tree to secure the rope."

From his saddlebag, Jason handed her what could pass for a towel, and a bar of homemade soap. She could have kissed him right there. "Is this why you got the rope, so I could take a bath?"

"We'll need it to cross the river tomorrow."

They walked along the deserted riverbank in search of a thick stand of trees sturdy enough to hold a rope, and dense enough to give Cassie cover while she took off her clothes. If anyone had told her when she left St. Louis that she would be disrobing on a river bank with a tall handsome man not twenty yards away, she would have called that person a liar. Yet here she stood, being instructed by Jason how to slide the loop over her shoulders to her waist before going into the water.

He tied it securely to a tree and walked away. "Yell if you need me."

Cassie quickly unlaced her heavy shoes, eager to submerge herself in the cooling water. Next her dress dropped to the sandy ground. She thought about letting her chemise follow, but couldn't bring herself to take it off when she knew Jason couldn't be far away.

She slipped the loop of rope over her shoulders and tightened it at her waist. She tugged at the rope to make sure it was securely tied to the tree and then walked into the swirling water.

*   *   *

The next morning the burning sun turned the cool air to fire before they devoured a quick breakfast of biscuits and coffee. Felipe and Jason repacked the horses, tying the supplies snugly in preparation for crossing the river. Losing their slim supply of food in the river would be a disaster they didn't need.

The sun sparkled on the swift, swirling water and Cassie shuddered. The river had to be at least a hundred yards across, but how deep? Jason had mentioned a sandbar. If the horses could keep a footing, the crossing would be reasonably safe, but if the animals had to swim, could they stay afloat with supplies and riders?

Jason strung the horses together by tying a rope around his waist and attaching it to the lead of Cassie's mount. He then tied the lead from Felipe's horse to the rear of her saddle. Cassie watched and worried. "You're not very sure of the sandbar, are you?"

"No, I'm not. Sandbars can shift in the current," Jason said, "but we have to get across." He coiled another rope and fashioned a loop on the end. "When we get close to the other side, I'll try to lasso a stump to steady us."

He motioned Cassie to mount the middle horse, with the saddle, and Felipe the third. "Hang on," he ordered. "If your horse loses its footing, the river could carry you away."

Cautiously, he led them into the churning water. His horse staggered at the impact of the current even so close to the shore. Cassie's mount swayed, then found a footing. She glanced back at Felipe. He grasped the animal's mane with both hands.

Step by step Jason led them into the fast, muddy water. Step by step Cassie's horse followed. The ten-foot lead between them gave Cassie little assurance. If Jason's horse floundered, hers would do the same, and so would Felipe's tied behind her.

Jason inched ahead. The water got deeper. The strength of the current increased, pulling at Cassie's thighs, belling her skirt to the surface.

Cassie worried with each precarious step of the horses. Here and there debris, tree branches, and now and then a good-sized limb zipped along with the current, displaying its speed. They were nearly to the middle of the river, but the other bank still seemed miles away. Water slapped at her waist. Her mount raised his head to escape the swirling water. She patted his neck. "Easy, fellow, we'll soon be across."

"Hang on with both hands," Jason yelled. Then his horse disappeared. Only Jason's head and shoulders stuck out of the raging water.

Cassie screamed. Then Jason's mount, with him still astride, reappeared, snorting and wet. Cassie's horse then dipped under the water, but at least she had had some warning. They had lost the sandbar.

She glanced behind her. Felipe and his horse were still together. The horses swam laboriously, trying to carry their heavy loads and keep their heads above water. Cassie's knuckles whitened where she gripped the saddle horn, struggling to stay on her mount.

She saw the huge limb coming down the river. Jason must have seen it too, because he urged his horse to go faster. A yell pierced the hot desert air. Cassie turned, nearly unseating herself. Felipe was gone!

"Jason!" she yelled. "Felipe! It hit Felipe!"

"I see him," Jason answered. Already the swift current had carried Felipe several yards down the river. He didn't seem to be fighting the water. Couldn't he swim?

"Felipe!" Cassie cried.

Finally Felipe raised his head and began struggling against the current.

Jason stood high in his stirrups. The swimming horse floundered. Jason uncoiled the rope and swung it through the air. The lasso dropped over Felipe's head, holding him against the current.

Slowly, Jason dragged the half-conscious Felipe toward them. Felipe's hand moved, struggling with the rope that encircled his neck. "Leave it on," Jason yelled.

Felipe obeyed.

Jason dragged him close and lifted Felipe up and across the neck of his horse, then slid back and held Felipe upright in front of him.

Cassie had never felt quite so helpless in her life. "Is he all right?"

"He's alive."

The minutes drifted by, each one an hour long.

Could Jason's horse handle the added weight of Felipe? Could they make it to the other shore?

An eternity passed, an eternity of Jason's horse struggling to stay afloat, of Cassie hanging on to her saddle horn with all her strength. What would they do if Jason's horse succumbed to the rushing river?

Cassie's mind raced. The horse she rode was lashed to Jason's waist. He would be safe. "Tie Felipe to yourself," she yelled. She watched nervously as he secured the end of his lariat around Felipe and then around himself.

Jason's horse staggered, seemed to stumble, then raised his head. Exhilaration swept over her. The horse had found footing. Jason raised his arm but she didn't need him to signal all was well. She knew they would make it across the river.

They neared shore, and Cassie slid from her mount and ran ahead to grab the bridle of Jason's horse, leading the exhausted animal onto the sandy beach. She raised her arms to Felipe, and Jason loosened the rope and let Felipe slide into Cassie's arms.

Carefully she lowered him to the ground. Blood trickled from a cut on his head at the crest of a huge bump.

Jason was soaked from his dip in the water, but Cassie's clothes were dry from the waist up. Without hesitation she ripped off her long sleeves, tearing part of her bodice with them. A thin chemise under her bodice covered her somewhat.

Expertly she folded the material to make a compress and pressed it against Felipe's head.

Jason tethered the horses to a spiny tree and unlashed a drenched blanket from a pack. He spread it a few feet from the water. "Let's get him out of the sand."

She smiled weakly up at Jason. "That was pretty fancy roping."

"I was lucky."

He stared at her thoughtfully. She turned her back to conceal her ripped bodice. He dug into his pack and wrung the water from a shirt, then tossed it her way. "It's wet but it will cover you up."

The moist shirt felt good against her shoulders, already hot from the sun. She buttoned it nearly to the top, then rolled up the sleeves until she found her hands. "Thank you," she said, without looking up.

She remained beside Felipe, holding the compress against his head. He opened his eyes and Jason came to stand beside him. "You picked a poor place for a swim," he said.

"And you chose a poor place to lasso me. I'd as soon drown as be hanged."

Jason grinned and shook his head. "Either is pretty permanent. I chose the less of the two evils. Anyway, I couldn't let you drown. We'll need every hand we have on the trail. The next two days to Corrizo will be a hard part of the trip."

"We can't travel yet," Cassie snapped. "Felipe may have a concussion."

Jason began spreading their supplies out to dry. "I intend to wait 'til morning."

"Morning! We can't leave that soon. Felipe needs at least two days of quiet rest."

"He'll get tonight. We have seven days of food, maybe less. The flour is bound to be wet and unusable. Keystone is our first hope of supplies and that is seven days' riding time. *We* can survive a few days on water if Corrizo Creek isn't dry, but the horses must have food as well as water if they're to carry us."

Cassie jumped to her feet and faced Jason squarely. "He could die if he has a concussion." Cassie knew she looked unimpressive with the oversized shirt hanging on her slight shoulders and her blond, half-wet hair straggling across her face, but she didn't care. Felipe could not be moved tomorrow morning.

"I traveled after a night's rest and lived through it."

"He's just a boy. You're a strong, vigorous man."

He studied her for several minutes. He didn't see the straggly hair or the too-big shirt; he saw a beautiful, warm-hearted woman who had felt very special in his arms.

CHAPTER SIX

*T*he next morning, cool air still bathed the desert when Cassie got up and checked Felipe's head. By now a huge bump had risen. "Do you feel dizzy?"

Felipe sat up. "Not much." He struggled to his feet. "I'm all right."

"You better be," Jason said. "We've got a hard trail ahead."

Cassie turned around to see Jason kneeling beside a circle of rocks. He dropped twigs on a budding fire. The sun peeked over the horizon, glistening on his still-wet hair. His clothes were dry. A crazy warmth coursed through her.

She brushed aside the feeling. "In this heat, Felipe will have to take it easy." Cassie moved to take off the shirt Jason had loaned her.

"Keep it on, unless you want to get that lily-white skin burned off in the sun."

Cassie's skin hadn't been lily-white since she'd boarded the wagon train. The sun had tanned it to a golden brown. It would never be white again.

She helped Felipe over to the campfire. "I am fine to travel," he said. He fingered the bump on his head. "It's only a little sore."

He strode down to the river, knelt, and cupped water in his hands and splashed his face. He returned to the campfire and reached for a tree limb to break up for fuel.

Jason stopped him. "I'll take care of that. Sit by the fire and tend the biscuits." Then he added, "I don't want to be held up by anything else."

Cassie smiled to herself. Jason wasn't as tough as he pretended to be.

They shared a hearty breakfast, and Cassie noticed that Felipe didn't leave any crumbs on his plate. She and Jason packed the horses and the three of them headed west.

They had traveled a mile or so before she noticed that the sand of the desert bore no wagon-wheel ruts or footprints. Anxiously she trotted her horse up beside Jason's. "Have we lost the trail?"

Jason's lips parted in a wry grin. "What trail?" His face sobered. "Cassie, there is no trail. We have a day and a half, maybe two, traveling west, and we will reach Corrizo. At Corrizo we will pick up the Gila Trail, and perhaps a wagon or two, if the bandits haven't frightened them all into waiting at Fort Yuma."

"But how will you find it," she asked, spreading her arms, "in this sea of sand? It's just a little river, you said. It could be anyplace."

"That's right, and we'd better move right along.

It surfaces at one point, then goes underground. We could easily miss it."

By noon the desert sun had scorched their bodies until Felipe slumped forward, exhausted, clinging to the mane of his mount. Cassie yelled at Jason to stop. "Felipe needs water and a few minutes' rest."

The water revived Felipe, and he silently chewed a piece of beef jerky. Jason rationed a piece to each of them, with a half cup of water. He removed his hat and put it on Felipe's head. Felipe had lost his in the river. "This will keep you cooler."

Felipe removed the hat and shoved it back at Jason. "I can take the heat as well as a white man," he snapped.

"Not with that bang on the head you got. We have neither the time nor the water to risk being held up by a rider who can no longer stay on his horse."

Angrily Felipe slapped the hat onto his head. "I will not hold you up," he said.

They mounted and plodded on through the killing heat. A lot of questions whirled in Cassie's mind. Why had the train been burned, and the people killed? All the supplies had been taken, but the bandits could have gotten them without massacring the people.

She glanced back at Felipe to make certain he was all right, then moved forward to ride beside Jason. "The bandits wanted our food and supplies, but they couldn't have needed them for themselves.

Fort Yuma wasn't that far away. Why did they want them badly enough to kill the people?"

Jason gazed her way. Bandits didn't usually kill everyone on a train. There had to be another reason why they had wiped out everyone on the wagon train, but he didn't mention that to Cassie. "To sell at exorbitant prices to immigrants who run out of food or have it stolen by Indians on the trail." He paused, then went on. "The jerky you ate an hour ago could have come from your own supply wagon."

"You knew them, didn't you, and you didn't even try to capture the men who killed my father."

"I didn't go into the camp after prisoners, I went to get food and horses." He smiled benignly. "And I had a pretty young girl and an Indian boy depending on me."

Suddenly Jason tensed. "Horses!" he yelled. "Go!" He swatted the rump of Cassie's horse, then turned and galloped back to Felipe. Grabbing the reins from Felipe's hands, he dragged the tired horse into a full gallop and caught up with Cassie. He pointed. "Get behind that rise. Get out of sight."

Sand pulled at the horse's hooves, turning the gallop into a labored trot. From the north an enormous cloud of dust rose into the stifling air. Cassie urged her horse faster.

Felipe demanded his reins from Jason, who slowed and returned them to Felipe's outstretched hand. No one asked questions; they just urged their struggling mounts through the sand.

When they got to the base of the rise, the hill of sand looked insurmountable. The horses tried, but drifting sand hampered every step. Cassie slid to the ground and pulled her horse behind her. The others did the same.

Sand seeped into her low boots, scratching her raw feet. Still she pushed ahead, leading the horse behind her. Nobody talked. Nobody asked questions. If Felipe knew what the cloud of dust indicated, he didn't say.

The grade became steeper. Cassie's parched mouth begged for water, but she dared not stop. Whatever the cloud of dust meant—horses and riders or something else—the danger must be great for Jason to order them to run. Just a few more yards and they would be on the other side of the dune, out of sight.

Deep sand dragged at her boots and dry, stickery brush scraped her bare legs; still she trudged on. Up, up, and finally, when she believed she could not take another step, over the top.

She ran a dozen yards down the other side, dragging her horse behind her, before she sank to the ground exhausted. Jason and Felipe joined her.

Wordlessly she reached toward the canteen secured on her saddle. Jason uncapped it and handed it to her. "Not too much at a time," he said.

She wanted to snap at him that she knew that much, but she was too tired. A few swallows removed the awful edge of her thirst, and she handed the canteen to Jason. Felipe appeared in better condition than she expected after the long climb up the hill. How could his people have called him a poor warrior?

"What are we running from?" Cassie demanded.

Jason secured the horses carefully to a washtub-sized rock, then came to sit on the sand beside Felipe and Cassie. "The cloud of dust means mustangs are being driven through by the Murietta horse gang. The animals are captured up north and driven into Mexico and sold."

"So why the mad rush to get out of sight?" Cassie asked. "All we really needed to do was get out of their way. You acted as though it were a matter of life and death. You're not very brave if you're afraid of a few men driving horses."

Felipe bristled, and Cassie wondered why. What had Jason done to earn such loyalty?

Jason glared at her angrily. "Those men have been on the trail for a long time, and there's nothing they'd like better than a young woman to share tonight. They're rough and cruel, Cassie, and they have a reputation for using women until they die."

Cassie shuddered, but she had to argue. "I've heard of the Murietta gang, but not the part about women."

"There's more than one bunch. Some are pretty decent, even helpful, I've heard, but the gang that comes through this part of the desert is a renegade group. They steal and they kill."

Cassie staggered to her feet. "Then let's get out of here."

"Not until they pass through. We'd be visible riding across the sand." Then he added, "And the horses need rest."

So did Cassie, but she refused to admit it. She lay back on the sand. What she would give for some shade from the blazing sun, but there was none.

She must have slept, because when she opened her eyes the sun had dropped behind the mountains to the west. She noticed that Jason still sat quietly watching. "Are they gone?" she asked.

"They're camping for the night."

She crawled across the sand until the herd of horses came into sight. Sentries circled the herd, keeping it together. Beyond the horses raucous laughter and jeering carried across the desert night. "Dare we build a fire to make biscuits?" she ventured.

"No," Jason said. "We'll have to settle for jerky and water."

"That's not very filling."

"If they see the smoke from a fire and come looking, you may have more than an empty stomach to worry about."

Felipe got to his feet and approached the drooping horses. "They must have water soon," he said.

"We've lost two hours today," Jason said. "The chances are good that the gang will move the horses early tomorrow to make use of the cool air.

If we do the same, we can be at Corrizo and water by tomorrow afternoon."

The next morning Jason shook Cassie awake. "It's still night," she complained.

"The sun will be up soon. The horse gang left half an hour ago."

By afternoon of the next day, they were afoot, leading their horses through the murderous heat. At noon they had stopped in the questionable shade of a stand of yucca and devoured a filling meal. The horses obediently permitted themselves to be led, but often stopped, reluctant to walk any farther.

Felipe urged them on. He seemed to have a way with horses, making them unrealistic promises of all the water they could drink and all the grass they could eat if they would just follow him.

Suddenly the horses picked up their gait. "There it is," Jason yelled, pointing to a row of trees in the distance. "There's Corrizo!"

They raced for the river. Now Cassie could see a wagon. They had reached the Gila Trail.

They were no more than a hundred yards from the river when a bullet whistled inches from Jason's head. They dropped to the ground. "Bandits?" Cassie whispered.

"I don't think so. I see a wagon."

The horses fought to get away. They had smelled the water. "Let them go," Jason ordered.

"Our supplies, our food!"

"We can't hold them. They need water."

The noise of the horses receded, and Cassie heard the cries of alarm coming from the wagon camp. "Keep them away!" the people yelled.

Jason got to his feet and called out. "Hold your fire. You have nothing to fear from us."

"I see an Indian," one of them said.

Cassie glanced behind her at Felipe. His long black hair gave him away.

"Stay close behind me, both of you," Jason ordered, and he advanced several yards.

"This Indian will not harm you," he promised. "We need water and a camp for the night."

Jason moved closer. As he advanced, two men and a woman formed a barrier to the water. Felipe made no move to dash back into the desert. He trusted white men more than he should.

A big man stepped forward, pointing his rifle at Jason. Another with a gun joined him.

Jason stopped. "We are coming in."

A child of about five clung to its mother's skirts. Cassie heard a baby cry. She noticed that only one horse grazed in the tall coarse grass. A wagon and only one horse? The people looked gaunt and hungry. How long had they been at Corrizo?

"You are not coming in," the man who appeared to be the leader yelled. "One more step and I'll shoot."

These were cruel men, turned killers from desperation. The man waved his gun, threatening to shoot. "We'll keep the horses." He glanced at the narrow river, where the horses stood ankle-deep in the cool water. The woman dragged the packs of food to the ground. "Two of the beasts don't look like much, but one seems pretty fair. Should be able to pull the wagon a day before they drop."

Cassie covered her mouth to keep from crying out. Behind them stretched miles of desert, hot and dry. Their small remaining supply of water, their food, their guns—everything—were strapped to the backs of their horses. They would die if they were turned back into the desert.

CHAPTER SEVEN

*J*ason got slowly to his feet, bringing himself a few steps closer to the rifle pointed their way. "Then what will you do?" he called out. "There's no supplies until Keystone. That's seven days away."

The woman had pulled the supplies from the horses and spread them on the ground. She dropped strip after strip of jerky into a pot. The small child grabbed at the food but the woman gently held him back. Hunger haunted both their faces.

Jason couldn't believe what he was seeing. "If you don't ration that food, you'll never make it to Keystone."

Gun still raised, the apparent leader motioned his partner to check the woman cooking the food. "We'll get more supplies off the next bunch that comes through," he barked. "We'll survive."

"Nobody will be coming, at least not for a week or two. They've been warned to stay at Fort Yuma or be robbed by bandits."

"It wasn't bandits who robbed us. Indians."

"And they left you guns and a horse?"

"We hid the guns. The horse is lame."

"How many immigrants do you plan to kill so you can survive?" Each time Jason spoke he moved a step or two closer.

"Many as I have to."

Jason still carried a Colt .44 with five rounds in the belt of his trousers, but all extra ammunition was in his saddlebag. If he tried to draw on the man holding the rifle, he could be killed. Cassie and Felipe would never make it to Keystone alone. He took a mental inventory. He had a gun with five rounds, and he knew Felipe carried a knife strapped against his leg. But without water. . . .

He paused for a long moment, trying to analyze the man who held the rifle. He appeared to be a family man. He would, without doubt, kill to feed his family. But most men were not eager to have the deaths of three people on their conscience. "At least give us water. Fill our canteens and give them to us and you can have the food and horses."

Behind him, he heard Cassie groan and Felipe tell her to be quiet.

For several long moments, the leader hesitated; then he conferred with his partner. It was the woman who seemed to force their decision. Jason could see her admonishing him with her finger.

Finally he turned toward Jason. "Back away. We'll fill your three canteens and lay them out there." He pointed to a spot in the sand fifty yards away. "Don't come near them until I say, or I'll shoot."

Jason nodded and directed Cassie and Felipe to back away with him. "We'll starve," Cassie whispered.

"Would you rather be dead?" Jason smiled tiredly. "I haven't got time to get shot. I have work to do."

"Oh!" Cassie wailed, and she stomped away.

They watched as the two men, rifles covering Jason and the others, approached the designated spot and tossed three canteens onto the sand. They backed away, then motioned for Jason to retrieve the canteens.

Quickly Jason picked them up, shook them, and nodded. They were all full. He removed one cap, tasted, then hurried back to Cassie and Felipe and handed each a canteen. "Just a couple of swallows, we've got a long way to go."

"We can't go seven days without food," Cassie said. "Even I know that."

"We will not die." Felipe pulled his knife from the sheath fastened to his leg. "We have a knife, Jason has five bullets in his gun, and we have water. We will make it."

Felipe's quick glance at Jason told him he was not so sure, but Jason only smiled.

Jason studied the sun. "We have about four hours until sundown. I haven't used this trail for a couple of years. We'll have to watch for a safe place to sleep."

Cassie looped the strap of her canteen over her shoulder and marched ahead. "I don't see anything but sand. Where is safe?"

Jason and Felipe followed. Each shook his head and smiled, as if to say, "Women."

"Safe is a rolling rise in the sand that we can camp behind, off the trail," Jason said.

The multitude of wagons that had used the trail had packed it firm. Even though blowing sand often hid parts of it, they had no trouble staying on the trail. For a time the three walked side by side. "When will the wagon trains dare to leave Fort Yuma?" Cassie asked. "Maybe one will catch up with us and have food to share."

"They will go when the soldiers tell them they can."

"Why don't the soldiers escort them?"

"That's not their job."

"I thought their job was to protect the settlers from Indians."

"The bandits are not Indians."

"That bunch that took our supplies said Indians robbed them."

Felipe interrupted. "If it *was* Indians, they'll feed their families with the food and trade the horses for guns. But I don't believe it was Indians. They would have searched until they found the guns even if they were well hidden."

Jason glanced at Felipe. "Have you been this way before?"

"Three times. It is the trail from my tribe at the Valley of the Springs near San Diego, to the river."

By sundown, the August heat had drained their bodies, and they climbed a rolling rise in the sand to make camp on the other side. "Two swallows of water," Jason instructed, "then we sleep."

All the next day, Cassie's stomach begged for food. By late afternoon of the second day, she became lightheaded from hunger. She noticed, too, that Felipe and Jason often wandered off the trail. She was too exhausted to ask why. Were they about to succumb to the heat?

The two were together off the trail when a gunshot jerked her back to reality. She staggered through the deep sand toward Jason and Felipe. On the ground a four-foot-long snake writhed helplessly. Its head was gone.

Cassie's stomach churned with revulsion. "I won't eat snake."

Jason grinned. "Then you aren't hungry."

Felipe flipped the dead snake onto a rock and expertly removed its skin and insides while Jason gathered dry cactus and built a fire.

In spite of her revulsion, Cassie's stomach responded to the smell of food cooking. When it was done, Felipe cut an equal portion of roasted snake for each of them.

Cassie watched as the others bit into the white meat. Hunger drove her to bite gingerly into the piece she held. It tasted mild and sweet on her tongue, almost like chicken. She noticed Felipe's smile when she took a second bite. Maybe he had been right; they would not die on the desert.

That night, sleep behind a low sand dune seemed less scary. She had food in her stomach and a small amount of water in her canteen. She had to admit, if only to herself, that Jason had been right. She and Felipe would not have made it across the desert alone. She refused to consider that they had five more days to go before reaching Keystone.

By noon of the fourth day, when they stopped to rest, Cassie's fear burst forth. "We need food soon," she said. She shook her canteen. "Nearly all my water is gone, and we still have three and a half days to go."

Jason nodded. "We'll camp before sundown and search for food. Maybe another rattler or a jackrabbit."

They found neither. Jason and Felipe were still talking when Cassie dropped off into a nervous sleep.

The next morning, long before daybreak, they climbed from behind the sand dune that had been their camp. Jason grabbed Cassie and Felipe and roughly jerked them back out of sight. The moon bathed the desert in a silver glow.

Jason motioned them to crawl up beside him. Below on the trail stood a wagon. Under it lay two men, and still yoked to the wagon was a lone brown stallion. "It's them," Cassie whispered.

A baby cried plaintively. "They're still alive," Jason said. "Stupid, but alive. Only a complete fool would try to bring the wagon. They have evidently lost the other horses, and the stallion can't pull the wagon alone."

"I wonder if they've got any of our food left."

"Five of them to eat. They could have a little if they rationed it properly."

Felipe stood up. "It belongs to us."

"Sit down," Jason ordered. "We don't want them waking up and shooting at us."

Jason put his finger to his mouth to silence them, then pulled the gun from his holster.

"No," Cassie whispered. "You can't shoot those people for food."

"I don't want the food, it's the stallion I'm after. If they try to make him pull the wagon alone, they'll kill him. I've grown pretty fond of that horse."

"You can't get the horse, they'll shoot you," Cassie warned. "Haven't you been wounded enough for one trip?"

"I recovered."

"There's no Tillie here to remove a bullet."

For several moments Felipe seemed to study the stars. "The horse will do us no good if we don't have food. I believe there is an Indian camp several miles to the east. They are hostile, but if they have food, I believe they'll trade it with me for guns."

"Even if you could get there, where do you plan to get guns?"

"You have a gun. I will use it to trade."

"A gun with only five bullets?" Jason shook his head. "Without a gun we will all be defenseless."

"Without food, we will all die. The night is still cool. I can cover a great distance before the sun rises."

"Are you sure there's an Indian camp out there?"

"I am sure of nothing, except that without food soon we will not get to Keystone."

Jason looked at Cassie, crouching silently beside him. Could Felipe be trusted to come back? With a gun and his remaining water, he would not have to share any food he might shoot with them. If he did find the Indian village, would they permit him to return with food to feed a white man and a woman? "This is your decision too, Cassie," Jason said.

For several long moments she considered the chance they were taking by parting with the only gun they had. Their only means of getting food, their only protection. Hunger gnawed at her stomach. The hunger won. "I trust him," she said.

Jason checked the bullets in his gun, then reluctantly handed it to Felipe. "How far to the Indian village?"

Felipe shoved the gun into his belt. "Ten, maybe twelve miles . . . if I'm right. I will run all the way."

"It'll be light in an hour. You can't run in the heat of the day. You'll never make it."

Felipe looped the strap of his canteen over his shoulder. "Stay here. I'll be back by nightfall."

Cassie and Jason lay behind the crest of the sand dune watching as Felipe moved quickly down the other side. They watched silently as he moved toward the trail where the wagon stood.

Instead of crossing the trail, he approached the wagon. "What's he doing?" Cassie whispered.

Jason clamped his hand over her mouth. "Be quiet. I don't know."

They watched Felipe move stealthily in the silver moonlight. He approached the stallion and clamped his hand over its muzzle. Slowly, silently, he removed the horse from the braces that held it. Still holding the stallion's muzzle, he led it into the desert in the direction of the Indian camp.

Neither Cassie nor Jason spoke until Felipe had put some distance between himself and the wagon. They watched while Felipe mounted and galloped into the desert.

Jason swore. "He fooled us into trusting him. He's stolen our horse and he's got our gun. We'll never see him again."

CHAPTER EIGHT

*C*assie's eyes stung with the threat of tears. She hadn't cried much in her lifetime, if twenty years could be called a lifetime. Instead of crying she had fought back. Now the fight had drained out of her. "The stallion will die galloping on the desert without water."

Jason looped his arm around her where she sat on the sand beside him. "Not in one day. Felipe isn't a fool—he'll pace the horse on the desert. Once he reaches the Indian village, he will have food and water, and he will be with his people." For several seconds Jason hesitated, then went on. "Cassie, I don't believe he'll come back."

"Then why did you give him your gun?" She brushed off Jason's arm, even though it felt good around her shoulders. "You don't trust anyone, do you? I think he'll return and bring us food, even if the stallion drops from lack of water."

"It won't. A wagon carries water barrels, and they likely filled them at Corrizo. I doubt that they

82

would deprive the only horse they had left of something as vital as water."

Jason stood up and held out his hand to Cassie. "The sun will soon be up. If we can find a wash, we'll have shade. We'll stay out of the heat for the day and go on our way at sundown."

"But Felipe told us to wait for him here."

"We can't take that chance. We need to conserve our strength and our water. Besides . . ." he added, glancing over the crest of the sand dune, " . . . if those two men under the wagon come looking for the stallion, I'd rather not face them without a gun."

"They can't prove we took it."

"Out here, they don't have to."

Reluctantly, Cassie got to her feet and followed Jason along the sand dune, out of sight of the trail. The soft sand and low brush tugged at her boots and sifted inside, scratching her already raw feet. "Can't we go down on the trail?"

The wagon family was up now and gathered around the wagon. "As soon as they go on their way, we'll check the wagon for water and fill our canteens. *If* Felipe returns, the stallion will need it too."

"You're not so sure that he won't, are you?"

Jason grasped Cassie's shoulders and made her face him. "The Indians are his people, we are not."

For several moments they watched the two men's obvious anger at finding the stallion gone. One followed the horse's tracks toward the Indian camp; then his shoulders slumped, and he returned to the wagon. "They'll have to walk and carry their supplies," Cassie said. "And someone will have to carry the baby."

Jason nodded. "At least they have food, our food. I should never have given Felipe my gun." He examined Cassie's blistered arms. "Come on, Cassie, you need some protection from this sun. We'll check the water barrels on the wagon after they are well on their way."

Cassie fell into step beside him. "Do you think Indians robbed them?"

"Felipe said it was bandits."

"Then how come the family is still alive? They killed everybody but me on our train, then set it on fire. If I had moved, they would have shot me too."

"I wish I knew. Bandits usually rob a wagon train and run. They don't waste bullets killing the people." Ever since he'd grabbed Cassie off the desert, Jason had wondered why they had totally wiped out the train. "Tell me about your father. He was a doctor, I know that. Who knew when he was coming?"

"Just Uncle Henry. He probably told his friends. After all, it's quite an occasion when a doctor moves to town."

"Was he carrying anything of value? A lot of money?"

"Not that much. He left most of it in the bank at home. Said he'd send for it if he needed it. It belonged to my grandfather. He was an importer. Pa didn't like using Grandfather's money. Said he could take care of himself."

"What about your Uncle Henry? Did he get half of the inheritance?"

"I don't think so. Pa said he was wild and got into trouble a lot; that's why Grandfather gave him money and told him to go west. I think Pa wanted to go with Uncle Henry then, but my mother wouldn't leave St. Louis."

By now the sun was creeping up the eastern sky, and heat pounded their shoulders. Jason found a wash. He shook his canteen. Nearly empty. He no longer felt hungry, and Cassie hadn't mentioned food since they had left the sand dune. But that didn't make food less urgent. Soon weakness would set in. They had to reserve every ounce of strength they had left.

"Felipe said he would return by nightfall. Will he be able to find us?"

Jason grinned and his cracked lips hurt. "I think he'll be able to follow our tracks." How could he blow her hope of survival? Felipe was an Indian. The chance that he would care enough to bring them food and water was doubtful.

Cassie crawled under the overhang of the wash. The delicious shade cooled her face and arms. She pulled her legs up under her to protect them from the sun. One at a time, she emptied the sand from her low boots and massaged the raw spots on her feet. Her stomach ached from emptiness, but the sense of hunger had disappeared.

She frowned at Jason, propped beside her, against the cool wall of the wash. Waves of heat shimmered above the desert. "Is this how it feels to starve to death?"

"Cassie, we have water. We're not going to starve." He removed the strap from his canteen and held out his hand for Cassie's canteen strap. "I'm going to make a trap."

"A trap for what?" She unbuckled the strap from her canteen and handed it to him.

"Maybe a rabbit. And when I'm sure the wagon family is well on its way, I plan to check the wagon for rope or anything we might be able to use."

"We can't carry much."

He took in the dejection in Cassie's voice. Her face, burned from the wind and the sun, must hurt unmercifully, but she didn't complain. Her cracked lips showed a speck of dried blood in one corner. Where, he wondered, did a woman, hardly more than a child, get the grit to withstand this kind of hardship?

Her clothes were torn, barely covering her, and her hair had turned to a mass of yellow tangles, yet she still believed that Felipe would return with food and that she would make it to San Diego. That Uncle Henry had better be good to her when she arrived, or Jason would personally horsewhip him. "Try to sleep, Cassie, while you've got shade. At noon we'll move across the gully to the other side of the wash and take advantage of the shade that'll form there."

"Are you going to sleep?"

"I'm going to try to trap something for us to eat, then check the wagon for water and anything we can use."

"Don't go too far away."

He noticed the uncertainty in her eyes and her effort to conceal it. It had been a long time since a woman had depended on him. He rather liked the feeling. "I won't," he said.

He formed a noose with the canteen straps and headed into the desert. He hadn't done much trapping, and never in the desert. Mountains and green pastures were his home. There he would be able to survive, but never had he ventured into the desert without an ample supply of food and a gun.

After the shade of the overhang, the rays of the sun felt hotter than before. For what must have stretched into three hours, he searched for anything he could catch for them to eat. Once he spotted a rabbit hopping through the sand. Jason found his warren and set the leather noose at the entrance. But the straps weren't long enough for him to get out of sight. The rabbit didn't come back.

About noon, he approached the abandoned wagon. The two water barrels each held several inches of water at the bottom. At least they'd have water. He drank all that he could safely drink at the moment, then filled his canteen for Cassie.

Inside the wagon he found two lengths of rope,

and in a corner, probably dropped by mistake, a pocketknife. He rummaged through a small pile of discarded clothing. There he found a dress. Probably too big for Cassie, but at least not torn to shreds. It would protect her from the sun in the daytime and keep her warmer through the chilly nights.

He jumped from the wagon, looped the rope over one shoulder, and tucked the dress under his arm. He found a dented frying pan and added it to his loot. Not a scrap of food had been left behind, but then he hadn't expected any.

When he returned to Cassie, he found her pressed against the sandy wall opposite the wash where he'd left her. A narrow strip of shade protected her face. She reached out to him and he shook his head. "No food, but I have water from the wagon, and a dress for you."

Hunger haunted her eyes and he looked away. "I tried to trap a rabbit, but it got away."

She drank from Jason's canteen, then reached for the dress and held it up. "It isn't exactly my size, but it'll do. Did you find anything else?"

"I found a frying pan and this rope." He dug into his pocket. "And a knife. If I can get a snake, we can skin it."

"Felipe will be back in a few hours. We'll have food." She turned her back and slipped the dress over her head, then let her skirt fall to the ground. She winced when the sleeves of the dress slid over her arms, burned fiery red from the relentless sun.

The large dress drooped on her slim frame, which was gaunt from lack of food. They had been on the desert for eight days, with only a portion of snake meat in the last four. How much farther would she be able to walk? They were at least three days from Keystone.

"We'll have to start walking again at sundown," Jason said. "Will you be all right?"

"Felipe will be back by then. We'll have food and we'll all be fine."

She seemed to have no doubts about Felipe. Jason didn't have the courage to repeat that the chance of Felipe coming back with food was slim. He not only had to persuade a hostile tribe of Indians to give him food to feed whites, but had to care enough to come back.

Jason glanced at the early-afternoon sun. The overhang of the wash gave her a good two feet of shade. He handed her his full canteen. "I'll fill yours back at the wagon. Stay in the shade. With the rope, I should be able to trap something we can eat."

The sun was far in the west before he snared an eight-inch-long lizard to bring back to Cassie. He returned triumphantly, even though he realized the lizard would give them only a few mouthfuls of meat.

The lizard gave them even less food than he had expected, and he insisted that Cassie eat most of it. The few bites of meat brought back pangs of hunger. He tried to wash them away with big gulps of water from the canteen.

At sundown they returned to the wagon to refill their canteens and start up the trail. He noticed Cassie's steps falter and his arm circled her waist.

The moon rose, bathing the desert in silvery light. Cassie's legs felt weak, threatening to collapse. She leaned heavily on Jason's arm.

Every few minutes she looked across the moonlit sand to the east. Would Felipe come? He'd promised to return by sundown. That had been two hours ago. Little by little hope dwindled away, and with it her strength. What would happen to her when she could no longer walk? Jason couldn't carry her, and he wouldn't leave her. Were they destined to die together on the desert?

Cassie took one step at a time, willing her legs to hold her upright. *One more step along the trail,* she told herself. *One step closer to San Diego.*

Her knees buckled. "I—I have to rest," she gasped. Only Jason's arms kept her from slipping to the ground.

Jason carried her several yards off the trail and sat her in the soft sand. She just wanted to sleep. He wouldn't let her lie down.

"Sit up," he ordered. He pushed the open canteen against her lips. "Drink."

For the first time, panic gripped her. She was too weak to walk any farther.

Her eyes searched the moonlit desert. Only vacant sand dunes met her gaze. She sagged back onto the sand. She no longer had the strength to sit up. "The moon is so beautiful . . ." she mumbled. "All silvery. . . ."

"Cassie, hang on, we'll make it," Jason pleaded. He turned and reached for the canteen. Then he saw it. Just a tiny speck in the distance, moving fast across the desert.

CHAPTER NINE

*J*ason rubbed a hand across his eyes. Did he imagine the rider coming toward them? The speck grew bigger. He jumped to his feet and waved his arms. It wasn't a mirage. "Cassie," he yelled, "look!"

"It's Felipe! It's Felipe! I knew he'd come."

Jason helped Cassie to her feet. "I guess you know Felipe better than I do."

Somewhere she found the strength to grab Jason's arm and hurry toward Felipe.

Displaying a rare smile, Felipe leaped from the stallion and untied the pack. "I have enough food to take us to Keystone, but we must stay out of sight."

"Out of sight?" Cassie reached for the pack. "Why?"

Felipe's face sobered. "Because the Indians are Pimas and I took back the stallion. I left while they were rejoicing over obtaining a strong horse and a gun to add to their arsenal."

"You mean you gave them the stallion and then stole it back?"

"I could not have made it back by nightfall on foot."

Jason frowned. "What are Pimas doing this side of the river?"

"I heard them talking. They took over the Indian village a few days ago. It was a renegade camp. The braves were off on a raid. The Pimas slaughtered the women and children, and when the braves returned, they robbed and killed them. That is why I was able to buy flour and dried meat with your horse and one gun." Felipe shook his head and Cassie saw the uneasiness in his eyes.

Jason insisted that Cassie sit down, and he handed her jerky from the pack. "Eat this," he said. "It will give you strength until we can build a fire."

Felipe handed him a chunk of Indian bread made from ground corn. "This is part of the meal they fed me. I thought we would need every scrap of food possible."

Jason broke it in two, giving Cassie the largest portion. He turned thoughtfully to Felipe. "Wonder why the Pimas wanted the camp?"

"They plan to wait there until the wagons are released from Fort Yuma. The trains will be loaded with fresh supplies from the fort. Even while I was there, two bands of warriors joined them. They plan to attack the wagons on the trail."

Cassie ate the last of her bread. She had savored

every heavenly bite. "I can ride now, if the stallion is rested."

"We will move up there off the trail." Jason pointed. "If we travel behind that rise, we should be out of sight."

Felipe nodded and handed Cassie the reins. "If they see us and realize we have no gun, they will kill without mercy."

"I've never run into Pimas, but I've heard they don't even try to trade with the people coming through, just rob and kill."

"They'll do anything for guns," Felipe said. "Guns give them power, even over other tribes."

For the next two days, Felipe, Jason, and Cassie traveled mostly after sundown to escape the desert heat. During the day they rested in the shade of a wash or any cover they could find to protect them from the sun.

They would make it now, Cassie felt certain. They had enough food and water to take them to Keystone. From there the trail led into the mountains. She could almost taste the water from a cool mountain stream and feel the heavenly shade the trees would afford. But they still had to face the desert for two days, maybe more, until they reached Keystone.

The morning of the third day, Cassie heard the plaintive cry of a baby. She crawled up the bank of the wash and scanned the trail. Two men, a woman holding a baby, and a small child sat huddled together on the trail. The morning sun beat down on them without mercy. The woman rocked back and forth, trying to comfort the baby.

Cassie scrambled back down into the shade of the wash and shook Jason awake. "Those people are down there," she whispered. "The ones who took our food. The baby is crying."

Felipe, awake in an instant, crawled over beside them. "They won't get our food this time."

"They still have guns," Jason said.

"They're out of food, I know they are," Cassie said. "I can tell by the baby's cry. If the mother has no food, the baby can't get nourishment from her milk." Cassie swallowed hard. "The baby will die."

"Or we will," Felipe said, "if they see us."

Jason watched the emotions play across Cassie's face. He didn't want the child to die either, but dare they take the risk of being robbed again? They must have left Fort Yuma in spite of the warning. Without an experienced leader, someone who knew the trail, they had been lucky to get this far. It was obvious they were so afraid of losing the trail that they camped in plain view of any renegade who might come by.

"If they have ammunition left, they might kill us on sight and take our food," Jason mused. "If we pass them by, there's a good chance we won't get to Keystone without guns for protection from the Pimas." Jason sighed. "They need our food. We need their guns."

He watched Felipe's gaze scan the rise on the far side of the trail. Was he expecting trouble from the Pimas? Felipe pointed. "An Indian scout is watching the family on the trail. He probably has seen us too."

Jason's glance took in the tiny speck in the distance. A mounted rider stood silhouetted against the sky. "I see only one, are there more?"

"We'll soon know."

Jason had fought Indians more than once, but never without a gun. He glanced at Cassie and recognized the panic in her eyes. How would he protect her without a weapon?

The speck in the distance moved down the hill. Jason could see the blowing sand stirred up by the horse's hooves. The heat and the morning sun blurred his vision.

He squinted to see better. Two more riders crested the hill and followed the leader. Jason kept one eye on the family on the trail. They had spotted the Indians coming toward them. "Cassie, stay with the horse," Jason whispered and rolled over the top of the sand dune. Felipe followed.

They scrambled to their feet and ran toward the immigrants. The family, obviously terrified by the Indians coming toward them, didn't turn around. Jason and Felipe slid to a stop and dropped to the ground behind them. An arrow plowed into the sand inches from the biggest man. The woman cried out and hugged the baby closer, then pulled the other child behind her back.

"Get down," Jason ordered. "Give me your rifle."

The man turned shocked eyes to Jason. "Where—" he began.

"Give me your rifle," Jason repeated.

The man hesitated, apparently confused.

Jason grabbed the barrel of the rifle and wrested the gun from the frightened man. The mounted Indians pounded toward them. Jason aimed and fired, and the lead rider fell from his horse. The horse and the two other Indians kept coming.

A second arrow pierced the shoulder of the other immigrant. Felipe grabbed his rifle and pulled the trigger. The blast threw Felipe to the ground. He picked himself up and aimed again.

A third arrow dug harmlessly into the ground at Felipe's knee where he knelt in the sand. "You missed again," Felipe said.

The two remaining Indians turned their horses, retreating out of rifle range. Jason waited, expecting them to charge again, but they stood back, obviously conversing. The wounded Indian crawled toward the crest of the rise. A mounted Indian reached out a hand and pulled him up behind him.

Jason aimed but didn't shoot. "Think they'll charge again?"

Felipe let out his breath. "Not riding double. They'll take their wounded home." For several long moments Felipe didn't speak; then he added, "But they'll be back—with help and guns. We'd better get out of here fast."

The baby whimpered. Jason lifted the other child in his arms. "Follow us behind the dune."

The woman's tired eyes brightened. "You'll help us? You'd help us after. . . ."

Jason didn't answer her question, just indicated Cassie, who was slipping and sliding down the hill through the sand. "Cassie says the children need food."

The tall man reached for the rifle Jason still held. Jason shook his head. "I'll keep the rifle." The man didn't argue.

Cassie ran to Jason. "Will they be back? How will we hold them off?"

"I don't know. We'll do what we can. Right now we need to get out of sight and get these kids some food."

Cassie knelt beside the sitting woman. "I'll carry the baby," she offered. The baby screamed when Cassie took it away from its mother. "Now, now," Cassie crooned, "you'll be back with your mama soon as we get up the hill."

The woman attempted to rise but fell back into the sand. Felipe held out his hand to help. She shrank back. "I won't hurt you," he said, and Jason smiled at the impatience in his voice.

Reluctantly she took Felipe's hand and permitted him to pull her upright. She reached for it again when the climb up the sand dune became more than she could handle. This time she smiled weakly when Felipe helped her.

Running ahead with the crying baby, Cassie led

them into the wash, where the stallion stood hidden from the trail.

If Jason expected gratitude from the big man, he didn't get it. "You stole our horse," he said. "We wouldn't be half dead from hunger if you hadn't taken our horse."

"Yes, you would, and the horse would be dead too. People like you have no business on the trail. You should have stayed at the fort until the Army said it was safe to leave."

"Don't tell me what I should do. We got this far alone. Another day and we'll be in Keystone. There's lots of food and water there."

"Another day? We're two, maybe three days from Keystone."

The man turned away. "Got to get that arrow out and bandage up my friend's shoulder. Then he's got to have some food, and so do I."

Jason turned from him abruptly. "Not until the woman and children have been fed. You will wait. We have very little food to spare."

Jason joined Cassie where she was mixing water and broken biscuits in a cup. Her eyes sparkled and he noticed her effort to suppress a smile. She handed the gruel to the woman, who carefully spooned bits into the baby's mouth. "My name is Mary, and my husband is Ben," the woman said, smiling, "and I thank you for saving our lives."

Felipe sat cross-legged on the sand beside the other child and broke off pieces of biscuit, handing them to the boy. "I'm Fred," the child said to Felipe. "What's your name?"

Felipe told him, and then Fred crossed his legs the same way Felipe had. "Will the Indians come back?"

Felipe frowned. "I'm afraid they might. They're camped in a village a half day's ride from here. By the time they get back with guns, we'll be ready for them."

Jason glanced thoughtfully at Ben, who had already gobbled up his portion of food. "How much ammunition do you have left? There were several rounds in the saddlebag for the Colt and rifle you took from us."

The man wiped a dirty hand across his mouth. "Think them killing Indians are coming back?"

"How much ammunition?" Jason snapped. "We've got two women, two children, and a wounded man. We have to make a plan."

"What about that Indian you got with you, will he turn on us?"

Irritated beyond words, Jason indicated Felipe and Fred sitting together in the sand. "Your family is eating the food that Indian supplied."

Jason checked with John, the wounded immigrant. "Can you travel by sundown? It's easier on everybody if we travel by night and rest in the heat of the day. Our water will last longer."

John seemed glad for Jason's help. "After your woman fixed my bandage better, the bleeding stopped. I'm fine to travel whenever you say."

Jason sat down in the sand beside him. "We'll take it slowly in the morning and keep our eyes open. The Indians know we have guns, more than one, and they may stalk us. We'll stay off the trail and out of sight. The going will be tougher and slower, but we have women and children to protect."

"I'll do whatever you say." John glanced toward Ben, who was sitting alone. "About that ammunition, we got plenty. All we took from you and some of our own." He reached for the pack he was using for a pillow, jerked it from under his head, and shoved it toward Jason. "Your Colt is in this pack. You take it now while you can."

With food the camp quieted. The baby lay snuggled beside its mother, asleep in the narrow strip of shade from the wash. "Felipe, will you take the first watch?" Jason asked. "Wake me in a couple of hours, then you can get some sleep. Those Indians could be back by sundown. We may have a busy night ahead."

Jason made his way over to Cassie in the shade of the wash. "Get all the sleep you can. It won't be easy traveling tonight with two tired children."

"What about you?" She moved over to make room for him in the shade. "Do you intend to go on forever without resting?"

Jason sat down beside Cassie, leaned his head against the rocky back of the wash, and closed his eyes. He needed sleep, but he needed a plan too— a plan that would get them all safely to Keystone.

Ben could be a big problem. If the Pimas returned, John couldn't use a rifle, not with his wounded shoulder. That left himself and Felipe to hold them off. Ben could shoot, but if he got a rifle in his hands, whom would he shoot?

CHAPTER TEN

*W*hen Felipe shook Jason awake to take the next watch, he leaned close to Jason's ear. "Keep your gun handy. Ben tried to steal extra food. Says he's hungry."

"So are the rest of us." Jason glanced toward Ben, who sat alone some distance from the others. "I'll watch him. Any sign of the Pimas?"

"Not yet."

"I'm not eager to give Ben a gun, but if the Indians turn up, we may have to. We'll keep an eye on him."

Felipe wiped the back of a hand across his cracked lips. "You watch him. I plan to sleep until sunset."

Jason picked up the rifle, checked that it was loaded, and took his place at the guard post. From where he sat he could see parts of the trail below and the long slope of the sand dune beyond. The late afternoon sun burned his scorched arms, and he pulled his hat lower to protect his face from the rays. But nothing could eliminate the discomfort of the unaccustomed beard he had grown. He'd be glad to get home and shave it off.

The sun was a ball of fire beyond the mountains when Ben left the shade of the wash and came toward him slowly. "I need more food," he complained. "I ain't had enough to eat for days."

"You'll have no food until tomorrow morning, when we stop for the day. Only the women and children and the wounded man will be fed tonight before we start."

"At least give me back my gun."

"No."

"What if the Indians come back?"

Jason didn't answer. If the Pimas came back in force, one rifleman wouldn't matter. Their only hope would be to outsmart them, and that wouldn't be easy.

Cassie awoke with a start when the baby began to cry. Mary rocked the baby in her arms, trying to quiet him. "I'm sorry he woke you," she said.

Cassie rubbed the back of her hand across her face and winced. Her raw, cracked lips made it hurt to speak. "We have to feed the children and John. He needs food to heal his shoulder, and you need food to feed the baby."

John came slowly toward them, obviously testing his strength. He sat down in the sand beside the six-year-old boy, Fred. "Give my portion to Mary," he said. "She's done without more than anybody."

Cassie got the fire going quickly and dropped a

few pieces of jerky into a pan, and measured a small portion of water from her canteen. "This will give the baby strength." She smiled weakly at Mary. "And you too. We'll save some of the biscuits for along the way. We've got a long walk tonight."

Cassie looked toward John. "Is Ben your brother?"

"Brother-in-law. Mary, here, is my sister."

By the time the sun disappeared behind the mountains in the west, they were on their way. Jason insisted that Mary and the baby ride the stallion, and he divided the supplies between himself and Felipe. Jason carried the pack containing the food.

Fred caught up to Felipe, walking beside him and trying to match him step for step.

Ben brought up the rear alone, obviously not concerned that his wife, Mary, or the children might need his help. Cassie shook her head in disgust, but said nothing. She'd seen men like him on the wagon train, men who thought only of themselves.

On and on they walked, often stumbling over the low rabbit weed that covered the desert. A slice of moon gleamed on the sand and a million stars lit the sky. The air seemed cooler than usual and Cassie fell into step beside Jason. "Are we climbing?"

Jason guided her around a boulder. "Haven't you noticed the greasewood is taller and the rocks are bigger? By tomorrow night we'll be in the high desert."

Jason paused and surveyed the long incline ahead. "Mary, do you think you can walk up the hill? We can't risk losing the stallion. If the Indians attack and someone is seriously wounded, without the horse we'd have to leave him, or her, on the desert to die."

Mary handed the sleeping baby to Cassie, then slid to her feet. "We'll be fine. It's cool, so wonderfully cool." Mary handed the reins to Felipe and fell into step beside Cassie. She took the baby back in her arms.

For a long time Mary plodded along without speaking; then she turned toward Cassie. "Before you folks came along, I thought we'd all die out there. Now I know we'll make it to San Diego. I have a cousin there. She lives with her family in a tent, and her husband has work."

"We'll make it, Mary. Never give up, at least not while we have Jason and Felipe to look after us."

The climb became steeper, the rocks bigger, until they were fighting for balance with every step. Mary and Cassie took turns carrying the baby. Felipe carried Fred on his shoulders. Jason and John walked side by side at the front of the weary group, but Cassie noticed that no conversation went on between them.

Long past midnight, they stopped to rest. Nobody talked. The slice of moon high in the sky gave scant light to the night. A coyote howled, and another answered.

On a hill opposite them a pebble tumbled down,

bouncing into the ravine below. Jason tensed. Felipe handed the stallion's reins to Fred and crouched low against a boulder. "Get down and don't move," Jason ordered. Everyone obeyed.

An arrow whistled by and glanced harmlessly off a rock above. "They're here," Jason whispered. "The Pimas have caught up with us." He pulled his Colt from his belt.

Ben grabbed the rifle lying on the rock beside Jason and scrambled behind the horse. Without even aiming, he fired at the opposite bank. The stallion reared. Terrified, little Fred released his hold on the reins. Felipe dove for the trailing reins, but he was too late. The horse raced down the hill toward the ravine.

Jason shoved Ben to the ground. "You fool! You've lost our horse."

Ben swung at Fred, but the boy ducked. Evidently he was used to dodging his father's blows. Tears ran down the boy's face. "I couldn't help it, Papa. The horse jerked and I couldn't hang on."

With his good arm, John pulled Fred beside him. "Leave the boy alone. It wasn't his fault."

Jason watched the stallion race down the ravine, away from them, but also away from the Indians. Jason strained to see by the scant moonlight. No mounted Indian followed the stallion. Perhaps none of them cared to risk being shot.

He directed Cassie and Mary to hide with the children in the wide crevice between two big boulders, then handed John a pistol. "Can you handle this with your left hand?"

"You bet I can. At least in the dark, we can see gunfire better than arrows."

Ben sat on the ground holding tightly to his rifle. "I won't shoot again 'til they're real close. I promise."

"You'd better not," Jason said, "or you'll be sitting with a rifle and no ammunition. Make every shot count."

Jason crawled over to Felipe. "How many Indians do you figure there are?"

"I would guess four or five," Felipe whispered. "They're young braves who want to make a name for themselves by bringing back guns. No seasoned warrior would permit a pebble to roll when he's preparing to attack."

"Helps to know that," Jason said. He motioned to Ben and John. "Spread out."

Jason watched the opposite hill for any sign of movement. Nothing. Where were the Indians? He glanced around, scanning the boulders that circled them. Nothing there either.

Suddenly wild whoops cut through the night. Guns blazing, a half dozen mounted Indians charged toward them.

"Now," Jason ordered. "Give them everything you've got!"

Jason aimed expertly. A brave fell and rolled toward the ravine. The moon disappeared behind a cloud and only the spurt of fire from the gun barrels showed them where to shoot.

When the cloud passed, Felipe spotted two Indians climbing up the hill toward them. They had taken quick advantage of the hidden moon. "There," he whispered.

He squeezed the trigger. One Indian rolled back down the hill. "One to go," he whispered.

Jason fired. "Where are the rest of them?"

The lone Indian kept coming. To Jason's left, a rifle exploded. Ben's rifle. "I got him," Ben said, and started to get to his feet.

"Stay down." Jason crawled over to John, who crouched beside Ben. "There could be more coming."

Felipe joined them. "Wait and see if they come down to pick up their dead or wounded."

"How long should we wait?" Jason asked.

"I don't know. They could be trying to surround us. If they don't make a move soon, either they're all dead or they've returned to their camp."

"Keep your eyes open. I'm going to check the women and children."

Crouching low, Jason hurried to the two big boulders. "Are they gone?" Cassie whispered. Mary rocked back and forth with the baby in her arms. Fred clung to Cassie. Even in the scant moonlight, the terror showed on his face.

"We don't know if they're gone, dead, or circling around to get behind us," Jason said. "We're waiting. Felipe thinks that if they don't show themselves soon, they're gone."

Cassie turned worried eyes to Jason. "You all right? The others? Is anybody hurt?"

"Everybody's fine, but don't move around back here. I don't want you to be a target in case they're waiting for us to make the next move."

For Cassie, waiting seemed worse than gunfire. She tensed at every sound, willing her eyes to pierce the dark night. The pistol in her lap, buried in the folds of her dress, represented the only immediate protection for herself and Mary and the children. If the Indians had circled and planned to attack from behind, her gun could mean life or death for the men watching the opposite rise.

Cassie picked out Jason crouched behind a boulder and Felipe kneeling at another rock several yards beyond. Between the two, Ben sat leaning against a boulder, obviously instructed to watch the rear. She wished it were Felipe guarding their backs instead of Ben.

Minutes passed, minutes that seemed like hours to Cassie. She tried to busy her mind by estimating how long it would take the Indians to circle in the darkness and get up behind them. How many would there be?

Beside her, Fred wiggled and pleaded to stand up just for a minute. Cassie held him down. "Do you want the Indians to see you?"

He turned his head in every direction. "I don't see any Indians. Where are the Indians?"

"Shh . . ." Cassie hushed him.

They waited. A coyote howled in the distance. Another one answered. For a second, Cassie relaxed the muscles in her tense shoulders.

She saw Felipe turn and scan the desert behind them, then assume his watch of the opposite rise.

Suddenly Ben jumped to his feet and fired. Cassie's arms tightened like steel around Fred so that he wouldn't wiggle free. She could see little but Ben on his feet in the darkness. A gun exploded. Ben staggered and fell to the ground.

Cassie strained to see through the night. Felipe and Jason were no longer crouched against boulders. They were gone. Her hand trembled when she aimed her pistol at the opening between the rocks. She didn't fire. She dared not move.

Gunfire shattered the night. One shot, then another. A cry of agony split the air, followed by a wild grunt that seemed almost beside her.

An Indian, his neck gushing blood, fell between the rocks where she and Mary hid. Mary covered her mouth, but didn't scream. She pulled her baby closer against her chest. Fred sobbed quietly against Cassie's arm.

The women waited in the dark silence. Not a pebble moved, not a boot scraped the sand. The sliver of moon shone on Ben where he lay motionless in the sand. Cassie wondered if he was dead. Mary's face showed no emotion. Felipe and Jason were nowhere to be seen. Cassie longed to crawl from the hiding place between the rocks so she could see more, but movement now could bring the Indians down on everyone. She forced herself to sit still.

Blood from the Indian seeped into the sand. She remembered her father's blood flowing away and she knew the Indian was dead. He looked so young in the sparse moonlight, about Felipe's age, and suddenly Cassie was glad Felipe had left his tribe.

For several long moments silence surrounded them. A few yards away, Ben groaned but didn't move. Every impulse told her to leave her shelter and help him, but Jason had told her not to move from between the rocks. She didn't.

She squinted through the darkness. A figure crawled toward Ben. It was Jason. Cassie held her gun ready. If an Indian approached she would shoot.

On the rise, several yards above where Jason crouched trying to help Ben, something moved. It came closer. Cassie could see only the slow movement. She aimed carefully and squeezed the trigger of her pistol.

A sharp cry cut through the night. She watched, straining through the darkness. The figure scrambled over the rise and disappeared. Had she wounded a mountain lion or a man?

Jason raised his head and looked her way, then raised his hand in a short salute.

For the first time in hours, Cassie smiled.

More minutes passed before Jason crawled to where she sat with Mary and the children. "I don't think your husband will make it," he said to Mary. "He's losing too much blood. Would you like to go to him?"

Mary handed the baby to Cassie. "No man should die alone."

Jason sat down beside Cassie and perched his hat on his knee. "That was pretty good shooting you did. Thanks."

She glanced shyly at Jason. He looked exhausted, and his lips were cracked and scabbed. "Tillie taught me well."

"That she did."

He motioned to Felipe and John and they crawled over beside him. "Ben will die, I'm afraid. Mary is with him now." Jason felt sadness for Mary. Living in San Diego without a husband would be hard on her, but her brother, John, would take care of her; he seemed a responsible sort.

Felipe shook his head. "I counted six Indians. We are lucky we lost only one man. Did you see which way the stallion ran? I'd hate to have him die of thirst on the desert."

"We're close to the mountain pass. I think the stallion will sense that there is water in the mountains." Jason smiled slightly. "Who knows, he may even find his way home."

Felipe stood up. "The Indians are gone. A few minutes ago I heard their horses galloping toward the desert."

An hour passed before Mary returned and held out her hands for the baby. "Ben's dead," she said numbly. "I'm so tired. Can we bury him in the morning?"

John sat down beside her and pulled his sister into his arms. "I'll take care of it, Mary. Try to get some sleep."

"He was a good man," she mumbled. "He did the awful things he did because he was scared of dying out here."

"I know," John soothed, but Jason noticed that John's words carried little conviction.

Jason got slowly to his feet. "Felipe, can you stand the first watch? I think we're fairly safe here for the night. Now that the elevation is higher, we'll travel by day. By tomorrow night we should be well into the mountains."

Once in the night Cassie heard Mary sobbing, but when Cassie went to her, she realized Mary was crying in her sleep.

CHAPTER ELEVEN

*T*hey buried Ben the next morning. John said a prayer. Mary sobbed and clung to the baby in her arms, and Fred clung to his mother.

How many men, Jason wondered, had died before they reached what they believed to be the promised land? Jason had been born in the West, but he'd learned long ago that the West was a cruel and demanding place and that only the strong survived.

He glanced toward Cassie and Mary. They would survive. They both had the strength the land demanded.

He gathered up his pack. "We must go," he said, "so we will reach Keystone by noon tomorrow. There we'll have plenty of food and water and horses so we can ride."

Mary looked back at the grave she had left behind, then turned and marched toward Keystone.

That night, when they camped, they ate the last of their food. Jason hoped he had estimated the distance accurately, or he would have some hungry people on his hands.

Before noon the next day, they met a half dozen friendly Indians on the trail. The Indians smiled and pointed to the north. "Keystone," one of them said, as if he knew where they were headed.

Jason bobbed his head and returned a smile. "Thank you," he said. "How far?"

The one who appeared to be the leader answered. "Not far."

After they had passed, Cassie caught up with Jason. "Soon we'll have fresh meat and potatoes," she said happily. "I can almost smell them simmering in the pot."

Everyone moved a little faster along the trail. They were in the high desert now, where enough rain had fallen to feed patches of grass along the roadside, and here and there a tree struggled to grow. A mountain breeze cooled the air.

By the time the sun had passed midday, signs of the town appeared: a tent pitched off the road in the shade of a scrub oak; a broken-down trail wagon waiting to be repaired.

A few hours later the travelers marched triumphantly into Keystone. They may have appeared bedraggled and hungry, but Jason sensed the triumph he was certain they all felt.

By nightfall, Jason had secured ample food and three horses to take them to San Diego. He talked to two men who knew the trail, and they assured him it was reasonably safe. They should have no trouble the rest of the way.

Up before dawn the next morning, they headed for San Diego.

In the mountains they found small streams for water, and John shot a wild turkey for fresh meat.

Eager as Cassie was to reach her uncle in San Diego, sadness enveloped her. Jason would accompany them most of the way, but soon he would leave them to go to his ranch in the mountains. Would she ever see him again? As the days passed she had noticed him watching her, looking away quickly when she turned.

Sitting around the campfire at night with the leaves rustling in the balmy breeze and the moonlight making lacy patterns on the floor of the forest, Cassie sensed a stirring of emotions she'd never experienced before. She wanted Jason to hold her close and tell her this wasn't good-bye, but he made no move to touch her.

She licked her cracked lips, then brushed her tangled hair from her face. She didn't want him to remember her the way she looked now, the way she had looked in the past weeks.

On the morning of the fifth day in the mountains, Jason packed all the supplies on two of the horses. He waited until Cassie had mounted one and Mary the other. "I must leave you now and go to my ranch. John and Felipe will take you to San Diego.

You should arrive by late afternoon. Do you know how to find your uncle's ranch?"

Cassie nodded, hardly trusting herself to speak. Saying good-bye to Jason was even harder than she had expected. "I'll find it. My father carried a letter from Uncle Henry with a hand-drawn map of how to get there." Cassie brightened momentarily. "He must have shown it to me a hundred times along the way. I know it by heart."

Jason jumped astride his horse and guided it beside Cassie's. Suddenly he grabbed her shoulders and kissed her soundly on the lips. "If you need me for anything, just ask for the Van Dyke place. Most anyone in San Diego can tell you where it is."

Before Cassie could answer, Jason turned and galloped away.

She touched her lips with her fingertips, and smiled. She'd see him again.

John lifted little Fred up behind Cassie, and Mary and the baby rode beside them. John and Felipe walked.

By late afternoon, they paused on a hillside overlooking San Diego. The town lay pressed against the waterfront, and the ocean sparkled under the late afternoon sun. "I will leave you now," Felipe said. "I will go to my people at the Valley of the Springs." He smiled at Cassie. "I will say what Jason said. If you need me, anyone can tell you how to find the Valley of the Springs."

When he was gone, Cassie brushed away a tear. Felipe had been a good friend. She glanced toward

Mary and John, noting the anticipation on their faces. Cassie pushed aside her sadness and squared her shoulders. "We've conquered the desert together—now let's take on San Diego."

John stood tall beside her. "We will take you to your uncle's ranch. A young lady shouldn't be riding these roads alone." He grinned sheepishly. "Even though I have an idea you can take care of yourself."

An hour later, at the end of a road indicating the Harper ranch, Cassie hugged Mary and John. "I'll visit you when we've all recovered from our trip. I know you'll do fine with your cousin."

Mary squeezed Cassie's hand. "Thank you for everything." She paused, then added, "Stay in love with Jason, he's a good man."

Riding down the road to Uncle Henry's house, Cassie felt alone for the first time in days. She hardly remembered her uncle; she'd been only ten when he left. She sat up straighter on her horse. If he were anything like her father, he'd be a good man. Bravely she slapped her horse's rump and galloped up to the door.

Her uncle had a fine two-story house, its white paint bright in the late-afternoon sun. What appeared to be a stable branched off to the right, and to the left a carriage stood in a shelter.

The ranch seemed strangely deserted. A straggly oak tree graced the yard, but only dry grass surrounded the house.

A young Mexican boy came running from the

stable. Silently he reached for her reins. Cassie smiled and dismounted. "Hello. Is Mr. Harper at home?"

The boy didn't answer, just frowned. He pointed to the door.

"Thank you," Cassie said, and she mounted the steps. No one answered her knock. She opened the door and slowly made her way through an entrance hall into what appeared to be a large dining room.

A man wearing a wide-brimmed hat and a rumpled dark suit sat eating at the table alone. He didn't look up.

"Hello," Cassie said. "I'm looking for Henry Harper."

The man turned and scowled. "I'm Harper. Who are you?"

Cassie tried to reconcile the dusty, bearded face with her scant memory of Uncle Henry, the laughing man-about-town she vaguely remembered. "I'm Cassie Harper, your niece, from St. Louis. My father, your brother, was killed on the way . . . by bandits. I escaped."

"Sorry to hear that, we could have used a doctor on the ranch. Sit down. You hungry? Want a drink?"

Cassie slid into the chair facing her uncle. How could a man show so little emotion upon hearing that his only brother had been murdered by bandits? "I'd—I'd like some coffee, please," she answered.

"Chin. Hey, Chin," he yelled.

A middle-aged Chinese man hurried into the dining room. "Yes, Mr. Harper."

"The little lady would like some coffee."

"Yes, Mr. Harper," he repeated, and disappeared through a door at the far end of the room.

After Chin had brought coffee and left the room, Uncle Henry wiped his mouth and leaned his chin in his hand. "So you're little Cassie. When your pa was killed, how'd you manage to escape?"

"I didn't move. I guess the bandits thought I was dead like everybody else. When they set fire to the wagons, I ran for the river."

"How'd you get across the desert? Did you find another wagon train?"

Cassie shook her head. "No. An Indian boy named Felipe and a man who'd been shot in the shoulder helped me. We almost didn't make it." Cassie shuddered. "I wouldn't try it again."

"Most folks wouldn't try it the first time. You sure it was bandits? Maybe it was Indians who burned the train."

"No. I heard them talking. They were white men. They took all our supplies and the stock, then set fire to the wagons. I intend to catch the men who murdered my father, and see them hang."

Uncle Henry glanced at her sharply, then looked away. "How's a slip of a girl like you going to catch them? Give it up, Cassie."

"I'll never give it up, Uncle Henry."

"That's up to you, but even if you could identify one of the men, you'd never be able to prove it."

He patted her hand where it lay on the table. "We aren't fancy here, but I'll have Chin make up a room upstairs for you, and I guess you wouldn't mind some hot food. You look like you could do with a bath. I'll tell Chin to heat some water."

"Thank you," Cassie said.

An hour later, Chin led Cassie upstairs to a bright, airy room. In the middle sat a tin tub filled with steaming water. Across the bed, undergarments and a blue-and-white polka-dot dress lay neatly on the patch quilt spread. Where did he get women's clothes?

Quickly she disrobed and slipped into the water. Heavenly, absolutely heavenly.

By the time Jason neared his ranch, his mind still dwelled on Cassie Harper. He'd never known a woman with so much grit, or one who felt as good in his arms. She'd be attractive once she got the dirt scrubbed off. He hoped her uncle would treat her right.

Why did the name Henry Harper sound familiar? He shrugged and rode up the lane to his home. His father, the judge, would probably know who Harper was. He spent more time in San Diego.

Jason's three "adopted" children, two Mexican and one Indian, raced to greet him. All three had been orphaned by gunfights or hangings. One by one he'd taken them in because they had no place to go.

Twelve-year-old Pancho got to Jason first.

"Hello, Pancho, José. Running Bear, you're limping, are you hurt?"

Six-year-old Running Bear grinned up at Jason. "I almost catch a coyote. I fall in canyon."

Jason slid from his horse and hugged the children one at a time. "Now go feed and water my horse. He's very hungry. I must see my father."

Pancho grabbed the reins. "Where did you get this horse? Your stallion came home. Your father was very afraid you were dead."

The door of the ranch house opened and a white-bearded man, gray hair flying, limped toward Jason as fast as his cane would allow. He clasped Jason's hand. "So you got home. It's about time."

Jason grinned. The old man permitted Jason's arm around his proud shoulders as they walked into the house. "I see the rustlers didn't keep you off your feet for long," Jason said.

"That bunch of dummies? If they hadn't caught me in the stable without a gun, they'd all be dead. I recognized one of them, works on Harper's ranch. You have any luck catching up with them?"

All Jason heard was the name Harper. "You talking about Henry Harper, with a spread in San Diego?"

"That's who I'm talking about, Hank Harper. Don't know why they wanted our horses—took four of our best. Must have had a long ride ahead."

The old judge dropped into a chair as if the walk out to greet his son had tired him a great deal. Jason frowned. Had his father been beaten up worse than he admitted? "They had a long ride, all right," Jason said. "I found them camped on the bank of the Gila River. Guess I got too close. I caught a thirty-eight in the shoulder. But I saw two of them I won't forget for a while."

The judge's alert gray eyes glanced at Jason's shoulder. "That why you were gone so long? Looks as if you recovered."

Jason accepted a cup of coffee and a sandwich from a smiling Leo, who was cook, housekeeper, and, for the past weeks, nurse to his father. Tall, lean, and weathered like most sixty-year-old ranch hands, Leo had kept house for them ever since he'd been thrown by a spooked horse. He was part of the family.

"I would have been home sooner but that same bunch fired a wagon train. I grabbed a woman running from the fire. I couldn't leave her at the river alone because a young brave was on our tail. I took them both to San Diego."

The old man eyed him shrewdly. "What kind of a woman?"

"Beautiful, or she will be once she gets the dirt scrubbed off."

"What about the Indian?"

"Took him with us. Just a kid, but a good shot. He said he planned to join his people at the Valley of the Springs."

The judge got to his feet. "Next week Harper comes before my bench on an assault charge.

Knifed a man in town and nearly killed him. I plan to get him for rustling horses too."

"How?"

"I don't know how, yet, but I'll get him and he knows it. That's why his man tried to kill me."

"I thought they were after horses and you just happened to be in the way."

"Don't you believe it. They grabbed the stock to make it look like rustlers."

Leo stepped into the room. "Your water is hot, Jason," he said.

Jason brushed his hand along his straggly beard. "So you think I need a bath."

Leo smiled. "And a razor."

Jason got to his feet. His shoulder hurt and he was tired and hungry for a decent meal. He squeezed the old man's shoulder. "I intend to get the men who rustled our stock and beat you up. I plan to see them hang." He held up his hand as if to ward off an argument. "Legally," he added.

Jason soaked for a long time in the tin tub. While he soaked, he thought about Cassie. So her uncle was Hank Harper. That made it awkward for him to call on her, if he happened to be in town. He missed her so much he felt as if he'd left a piece of himself in San Diego.

Why had Hank Harper sent his ranch hands after the wagon train? He might rustle a few cattle now and then, but why go that far from San Diego to wipe out a wagon train, unless he was the one who was attacking the trains, instead of the Mexican bandits who were being blamed for it.

Jason lathered his face and picked up his razor. "Ouch." He wasn't convinced. Everybody, including the soldiers stationed at Fort Yuma, swore it was Mexican bandits.

As he dressed, he searched for a reason to go to San Diego to make sure Cassie was all right. He sighed. He planned to go to San Diego, all right, but not to Cassie. First he had to find the men who had nearly killed his father. Maybe, just maybe, they were also the ones who had burned Cassie's wagon train.

CHAPTER TWELVE

*C*assie lathered the clean-smelling soap over her body and soaked in the tub until the water cooled. Chin, who was obviously Uncle Henry's houseman, had even supplied a jar of soothing salve for her sunburned face and cracked lips. The clothes that she had found laid out on the bed hung on her slim frame, but they were clean and whole.

Uncle Henry puzzled her. He had seemed more angry than sad that she was alone. Maybe he'd wanted a doctor on the premises more than he'd indicated in his letter to her father.

At dinner that night, her uncle seemed jovial. "Chin," he told the houseman, "find a dressmaker for Cassie. A pretty young girl needs clothes that fit."

"Yes, Mr. Harper."

"I want to show you off to all my friends, Cassie. I want them to meet my beautiful niece."

Cassie glowed under his compliment. Uncle Henry hadn't changed. He still knew how to make her feel special.

The next morning a smiling woman of about forty, Mrs. Nelson, appeared at the ranch house. "I am here to see that you are properly dressed."

Cassie led her to her room. "I lost everything I owned when the wagon train burned. Thank you for coming to my rescue."

"Mr. Harper says you are to have proper clothes for a lady."

That night at dinner, when she tried to thank her uncle, he waved her gratitude aside. "If there's anything else you need, just ask."

Maybe she'd misjudged Uncle Henry. He'd seemed so cold at first. Maybe that had been his way of grieving for his dead brother. "I'd be pleased if I could have a horse to ride," Cassie told him. "I met a woman with two children on the trail and I'd like to visit them in San Diego."

"Tell Chin what you need. He'll arrange it."

The next morning Chin tapped on Cassie's door. "If you will go to the stable, Miss Cassie, the stable man will help you choose a horse." He paused before he continued. "Do not let him give you the stallion. You would be wise to insist on a mare named Penny. She will be gentle with you."

Cassie grinned. "Thanks for the warning, Chin."

Chin's smile warmed Cassie's heart. She had found a friend. This crazy household perplexed her. Uncle Henry ignored her most of the time, then seemed to do his best to be obliging.

When she was offered the stallion, temptation almost got the best of her. Her father had taught her to ride almost anything on four legs. But caution won, and she chose Penny, the mare.

Cassie spent the next three days making friends with the mare, patting her and talking to her, and bringing her treats. On the morning of the fourth day, they ventured out on the range.

Cassie wore a brown split skirt she had insisted Mrs. Nelson make for her, and an ivory silk shirt. With the wind in her hair she rode away from the corral onto the range.

Here and there a few steers grazed and several horses watered at a tank. Apparently her uncle was partial to horses. Urging Penny into a gallop, Cassie headed for a wooded area in the distance. Here she found eucalyptus trees mixed with live oak, and a fence.

For nearly two hours Cassie rode on the range, enjoying the September sun on her face and the wind in her hair. For the first time since the fire she felt unworried and free. Her father would have loved riding here. In St. Louis it was he who had insisted she learn to ride astride when they galloped through the fields.

She noticed a lone rider in the distance. He sat tall in the saddle. Her thoughts switched to Jason and her contentment flew away. When would she see him again?

She must have been fifty yards from the fenced timber when a shot rang out in the stillness. She wheeled her horse. Her chin smarted. When she touched it, blood covered her fingertips. The bullet had grazed her chin!

Instead of fear, anger exploded inside her. Something moved in the trees. Cassie kneed Penny into a gallop toward the woods. Without hesitation the mare cleared the fence and raced through the trees, obviously in familiar territory.

In the distance the rider sped across a narrow clearing. Cassie urged Penny ahead, but Penny was no match for the speed of the rider. If he was an Indian he wasn't dressed like one, but Cassie couldn't get close enough to see his face.

Finally Cassie slowed Penny to a walk and turned back toward the ranch house. Why would somebody want to shoot at her? Did someone think she was trespassing? The shooting and death on the wagon train flooded back to her, and she trembled. Out here there was no Jason to rescue her and she had no gun to protect herself.

Back at the ranch, she walked slowly into the house. No one was around. She made her way to the kitchen and sat in a chair at the small wood table. "Chin, I need a cup of coffee and some anti-septic."

Chin turned quickly from the sink. "Antiseptic? You are hurt?"

"Somebody shot at me and barely missed." She said it calmly, as if she were talking about somebody else.

He filled a cup and set it before her. "You were

out riding on the range? Perhaps you were mistaken for someone else."

Cassie sipped her coffee. "I chased him but he got away. If I had had the stallion. . . ."

He pushed a container of alcohol and a clean folded cloth toward her. "If you had been riding the stallion, you would be trampled on the ground by now, Miss Harper."

"Call me Cassie, Chin. Nobody has called me Miss Harper since I attended a snooty finishing school in St. Louis. I hated it."

"You prefer being shot at?"

"No, but I'd sure like to know who did the shooting. I need a gun, Chin. Is there a pistol around here that I could use without upsetting my uncle?"

Chin gazed at her thoughtfully. "You know how to use a pistol?"

Cassie dabbed alcohol on her chin and winced. "I certainly do. How do you think I got across that desert?"

"I believe I can find you one that will not be missed."

That night at dinner, the first thing Uncle Henry mentioned was the mark on Cassie's chin. "What happened to you?"

She hadn't planned to tell him, but she couldn't lie. "I was riding today and a man in the trees shot at me. I couldn't catch him."

"I should hope not. Don't tell me you tried."

"Of course I tried, but he had a head start and a faster horse."

He shook his head as if in dismay. "I hope those Indians aren't back. Killed three steers and dragged them away. We usually keep a guard out there."

Suddenly Cassie felt very foolish. Had she chased a man who was guarding the cattle? Had the dangers she'd encountered crossing the desert made her suspicious of everyone?

The following day Cassie decided she would be wise to stay off the range until her uncle could tell his guard not to shoot at her. She mounted Penny and headed into San Diego to visit Mary and the children. Mary's directions had been explicit, and Cassie had no trouble finding "D" Street and following it until she came to a cluster of abodes, half canvas, half wood, that looked as if they'd been thrown together to keep off the sun and rain.

Mary greeted her with open arms. Even little Fred seemed glad to see her. Mary led Cassie into her lean-to. "We saw Jason in town early yesterday. I reckon he stopped by your place."

"No. . . . No, he didn't," Cassie said, and her heart did a painful flip.

Mary squeezed Cassie's arm. "Oh, I'm sorry, Cassie, guess I shouldn't have mentioned it, but I was so sure. . . . He asked if I'd seen you. Wanted to know how you were getting along at your uncle's place."

Cassie stifled the unhappiness that surged through her. "I'm getting along fine, just fine." She couldn't tell Mary she'd been shot at; it would only worry her. Why hadn't Jason stopped? Had he forgotten so quickly, or hadn't there been anything in his heart to forget?

Another week passed, and still Jason hadn't stopped at the ranch. At night, when she was alone, she longed for Jason, but in the daytime, events at the ranch kept her too worried to think of him.

Now and then Cassie ventured onto the range, but carefully.

After one of the hands accosted her outside the stable, she carried the light .22 Smith & Wesson pistol that Chin had given her. She rather doubted that the ranch hand would bother her again—at least not until his broken arm healed. . . .

She'd been astride Penny, ready to leave for a ride, when Will, one of the hands, had grabbed the Ballard rifle from the scabbard of a saddle leaning against the barn. Without appearing to, she had watched him grab it by the barrel. When he swung the butt at her, apparently trying to knock her to the ground, she'd ducked, and the blow had glanced off the saddle. Her mistrust of everyone had probably saved her life.

Afterward Cassie had jerked up on the reins. Penny reared, knocking the man to the ground. Cassie released the reins. Before her assailant could roll away, the horse's hooves came down on his chest and arm. The man howled in pain. Cassie then turned her horse and raced away.

Galloping across the range, Cassie had tried to put together a reason for the frightening things that were happening. Will had never spoken a word to her, yet he had tried to kill her. And the rifle bullet that had nicked her chin had been meant for her head, she had no doubt of that.

That evening Cassie changed and dressed for dinner, still wondering why Will had tried to knock her off her horse. Thoughtfully she made her way down the shadowy steps to the dining room, but she stopped abruptly in the doorway when she saw Will, with his arm in a sling and his back to her, talking with her uncle. "That little w-w-witch tried to trample me to d-death."

Cassie felt the color drain from her face. The stuttering bandit! The man who had emptied her father's pockets, then torched the wagon. Her face had been covered with a shawl that day, but she would never forget that voice. No wonder he never spoke to her!

Cassie didn't hear her uncle's answer, just the pounding in her head that screamed, *Beat him, scratch his face until the blood runs in his eyes, kill him.* She tightened her small hands into fists, striving to control the hate that surged over her.

Through a haze of fury she saw her uncle pat Will's shoulder. "Take care of that arm."

Uncle Henry noticed her then. "Cassie, don't stand there, come in to dinner. Will is leaving."

Somehow Cassie made her legs carry her into the dining room. Will walked past her and the naked hate in his eyes sent a shiver through her body.

She took her place at the table and stared at the

setting before her. How could she calmly eat when her world was disintegrating? Clenching her hands in her lap, she spoke. "Will tried to knock me off my horse. I think he was trying to kill me."

"Kill you? Don't be ridiculous. You're a pretty girl, he was probably trying to kiss you. Boys will be boys." His teasing tone disappeared. "I think you were pretty hard on him. Now he's no good to me until that arm heals."

"No good for what?"

Cassie could feel her uncle bristle. "As a ranch hand, what else?"

She wanted to scream at him that Will was a bandit, that he'd burned the wagon train, but she kept silent. She had no good reason to be suspicious of her uncle, but she trusted no one. No one except Jason and Felipe.

Early the next morning, she saddled Penny and headed for the sheriff's office in San Diego. Jason had mentioned once that the sheriff was an honest man. Well, she'd give him a try.

Minutes after she left the ranch, she noticed a rider a good distance behind her. She quickened her pace, then scolded herself for being so suspicious. He could be anyone going into San Diego. When she neared town, the rider had disappeared.

When she arrived at the sheriff's office, second thoughts kept her silent about the rifle shot and the episode with Will. She had no real evidence, and her uncle would be furious if he learned she had gone to the sheriff. "I just wanted to report that a wagon train was burned and everyone was killed," she told the sheriff. "Everyone except me."

He nodded and spoke kindly. "Jason Van Dyke already reported it. I'm sorry you lost your father in the fire. Van Dyke said there was a possibility the bandits might be from around here."

"He did?"

The sheriff smiled at her surprise. "We're watching and listening for any loose talk in town."

Cassie got to her feet. "Thank you," she said, then asked, "Did Jason tell you that today?"

"No, a week or so ago. Last time he was down from the ranch. Doesn't come to town often, just wanted to tell me to keep a close eye on his father next week when he's on the bench. The old judge has a lot of enemies." The sheriff smiled. "With good reason. He's put a lot of bad ones behind bars."

Cassie thanked him again. Before she reached the door, she turned. "Sheriff, can you tell me which road to take to the Valley of the Springs?"

He frowned at her question, but pointed east. "Follow that street east. It runs into the trail. That's a long way to travel, young lady."

Cassie grinned. "It's a long day. I'll find it."

Outside the sheriff's office, Cassie mounted Penny and headed east. Several times she glanced back. She saw no one behind her on the trail.

For most of an hour she rode east, enjoying the morning sun warm on her face. She turned in her saddle to watch a sea gull swoop toward the bay.

That was when she saw the rider, the same one who had followed her from the ranch, not two hundred yards behind her.

Terror gripped her. Her hands shook. Out in the open, she didn't stand a chance against a fast horse and an expert rifleman—and if he was the same man who shot at her on the range, he *was* an expert.

She felt for the Smith & Wesson in the pocket of her skirt. A pistol would be useless against a rifle. Urging Penny into a gallop, she headed for a stand of trees in the far distance.

Penny responded neatly, but, glancing back, Cassie could see the rider, head down, gaining on her. In the trees ahead a movement startled her, then another. Riders in the trees.

Anyone watching could see she was being chased, so why didn't they help her? Were they friends of the man pursuing her, ready to surround her?

Still she headed for the grove. She had to take the chance that they were friendly. Head down against Penny's mane, she urged the horse forward. "Faster, Penny, faster." The grove seemed miles away.

For just a moment she raised her head. A bullet whizzed by. She was in rifle range of the man behind her, and he was closing in.

From the trees ahead, a rider showed himself. The sun glimmered on his bare copper chest. An Indian. Three, maybe four more figures moved around in the trees. Cassie looked back. The rider behind her appeared to have lost ground. Was his mount tiring, or did the threat of the Indians deter him?

Cassie headed straight for the men in the trees. If they were Indians from the Valley of the Springs, Felipe had told her they were friendly to whites.

She glanced again toward the trees. She was almost there, but the Indians were gone. Behind her, she could hear the rider pounding closer and closer. The trail grew slimmer, nearly obscured by low brush. A hidden rock could throw her and Penny to the ground.

When at last she plunged into the grove of trees, she slowed Penny. Cassie looked back. Her pursuer was coming fast. Cassie guided Penny deeper into the grove. A shot thudded into a tree beside her.

There was no way she dared gallop Penny through the dense eucalyptus grove; they would both be thrown to the ground. Backing Penny behind the trunk of a big tree, Cassie gripped her pistol and aimed at the oncoming figure. Her hand trembled.

Not twenty yards away, the man reined in his horse and stopped. It was Will, the stuttering bandit. His hand moved to his holster. Penny pulled the trigger of her Smith and Wesson. His holster jumped where the bullet hit.

Will jerked back his hand. Slowly he backed his mount out of the trees. Then he turned and raced away, head down.

Cassie's hand quivered so she could hardly hold her gun. Weakness sagged her shoulders, and tears streamed down her face.

When she looked up, a half dozen Indians surrounded her. The one who appeared to be the leader smiled. "Gone," he said. "Good shot."

Cassie smiled weakly. "Lucky shot." To hide her show of weakness, she mopped up her tears and straightened her shoulders. "I have come to see Felipe," she said.

The Indians looked from one to the other. "Felipe. Felipe," they repeated.

"Yes, Felipe. He said I could find him at the Valley of the Springs." Her words didn't seem to register. Couldn't they understand? She pointed to herself. "I find Felipe."

The young leader seemed to understand. He pointed toward the east. "Felipe hunt food."

"When will he be back?"

"Back? Back?" the young Indian said.

Cassie shook her head in confusion. "Tell Felipe, come to Cassie. A—a—" How could she make him understand the urgency? "Cassie in danger," she said.

The Indian seemed to understand that. He nodded. "Cassie, danger."

Cassie smiled and nodded, and then turned Penny toward San Diego.

The young Indian said something in his native tongue and two braves joined Cassie on the trail. "Danger," one of them said. Again Cassie smiled and nodded, glad not to be alone on the trail. But had she made their leader understand that she needed Felipe?

When they arrived at the edge of San Diego, the two braves stopped. "We go," one said, and Cassie thanked them profusely, even though she doubted they understood her words.

For several moments, Cassie watched the braves on the trail, then turned to go home. But she couldn't go home; Will could be there. How could she convince Uncle Henry that Will had tried to kill her?

Cassie reined Penny in and looked toward "D" Street, where Mary and John would be. Would she endanger them by going there? She had to take that chance. If Felipe came looking for her at her uncle's ranch and didn't find her, would he think to look for her here?

Mary's joy at seeing her vanished seconds after she opened the door. Obviously Cassie's fear was reflected on her face. Mary pulled Cassie into the house. "Cassie, what's happened? You're scared to death."

"Mary, somebody tried to kill me."

Mary drew Cassie into her arms to comfort her. "Why in the world would anyone want to kill you? You have your uncle to protect you. No one would dare." She released Cassie and led her to a chair. "Now, what happened?"

"It's the bandit, the one who stutters. He works on my uncle's ranch, and he knows I recognized him. Two days ago he tried to knock me off my horse with the butt of a rifle. I trampled him. I think I broke his arm."

"Didn't your uncle fire him when you told him what happened?"

Cassie shook her head. "He said Will was just trying to kiss me."

"You're a pretty girl. Maybe your uncle was right."

"No, my Uncle Henry was wrong. He didn't even scold the man. Then today I rode to the Valley of the Springs to find Felipe, and Will followed me and shot at me twice. He missed both times."

"Maybe he's just a bad shot."

Cassie pointed to the small mark on her chin. "Last week he did this at fifty yards."

"Are you sure it was Will following you today?"

"Yes. I saw his face when I shot him."

Mary paled. "Did you . . . kill him?"

"No, but I blew a hole in his holster."

"Oh, Cassie, he could have killed you! Does Jason know?"

"Jason didn't stop to see me the day he came to town."

"Maybe John will know how to find Jason. He found work on a fishing boat. He'll be home in three or four days."

"No! Felipe will help me. I asked a young brave to tell Felipe I needed help. Felipe will come."

"Cassie, you need a man to help you, not a boy."

By now Cassie felt a little foolish over the uproar

she'd caused. More than one man in this world stuttered, and at the fire, she hadn't seen the bandit's face. She smiled at Mary. "Now let's have a cup of tea. I want to hear everything you've been doing."

Mary poured tea and brought small cakes to the tiny plank table. "If the catch is good, John says we'll buy a piece of land and he will build a house for us. This is a glorious place, Cassie. I hear it never snows, even in winter."

Little Fred came in from playing and sat close beside Cassie, telling her about his new friends. Then he went back outside to play. Cassie and Mary talked for hours, until the sun dropped into the ocean and darkness approached.

When Mary called Fred in for dinner, he slipped into his place at the table. "A man on a horse been sitting up on the road for a long time. Do you think he's hungry?"

Cassie's fork stopped halfway to her mouth. "What does the man look like, Fred?"

Fred shrugged. "Just a man. Maybe he's looking for somebody."

Cassie glanced at the uneasiness on Mary's face. "I'm leaving, Mary. I don't want to bring you trouble. Fred, please bring Penny around back."

"You can't go. He'll follow you."

Cassie felt for the pistol in her pocket to make certain it was there. She hugged Mary and opened the canvas at the back of the lean-to. "Let him follow me. I'm going to the sheriff's office."

Cassie led Penny between the makeshift houses to the street behind. Twilight had become darkness before she mounted Penny and headed toward the sheriff's office. Glancing behind her, she saw that the road was completely deserted, except for a man on a horse who followed her down the street.

Cassie quickened her pace. She rounded a corner, intending to dismount and run in and ask the sheriff for help. All the shops were closed for the night. Not a single pedestrian strolled down the street.

She reined in Penny. The rider behind her came around the corner. Weakness, triggered by fear, engulfed her. The sheriff's office was dark.

Far down the street, in the opposite direction, the shadow of a mounted rider appeared; then, as quickly as he'd shown himself, he melted away between two low wooden structures. Had she only imagined him?

Behind her, the man who had been following her advanced. It had to be Will, the stuttering bandit. Now he was no more than two hundred yards away.

Frantically, she glanced in both directions. The only way Will could keep her quiet about burning the wagon train was to kill her. Trapped between Will and the man in the shadows, she realized the only escape from the street lay in the opening where the shadowy man had disappeared.

Cassie kneed Penny into a gallop and headed straight for the opening. Behind her, hooves pounded the street. She glanced back. Will's powerful stallion gained on her. Panic rose in her throat, but she forced it down.

She rounded the building at a full gallop. If someone waited to grab her, he'd have to catch her first.

Seconds later a rider rode up behind her. "Follow me," he called out, and passed her skillfully.

She raised her panic-stricken eyes to the rider. His broad coppery back gleamed in the scant moonlight. An Indian, but who? Not Felipe—she'd know his slight frame anywhere. Without question, she followed the rider through the dark alley.

Behind them, Will's horse seemed to slow as if he were looking for her. Suddenly the Indian wheeled his mount, grabbed Penny's rein, and pulled her into the darkness behind a store. He didn't speak. Cassie couldn't. Fear held her tongue.

Will galloped past them down the alley. Still they waited silently.

The hoofbeats of Will's horse faded into the distance before the Indian stepped into the moonlight. Cassie gasped. "You are one of the Indians who took me back to town."

"My name José. Man follow you. I follow man."

"Where is Felipe? I have to find him."

José released Penny's rein. "Felipe come soon, follow me."

Without question, Cassie followed José. Felipe had sent him; that was all she had to know.

She followed him to the waterfront, where rows

of plank board shacks hugged the sandy beach. Behind a shipping company, barrels containing she knew not what lined a platform. A long dock jutted into the bay, accommodating a tall-masted schooner. Several small fishing boats bobbed quietly in the moonlit water. Night had hushed the city to a standstill.

José halted on the sandy beach under the pier. He motioned Cassie to follow him between the log pilings that held up the dock. "We wait here for Felipe."

"Will he know where to find us?" Cassie realized that her question was foolish, and also that José could understand very little of what she said.

José smiled and shook his head.

His smile relieved the tension. For the first time since she had been shot at on the range, Cassie was not afraid. Now she was among friends. Soon Felipe would come, and between them they would decide what to do. She was no longer alone. Cassie dismounted and waited, silently content, for Felipe to arrive.

Time passed. Cassie leaned against a piling and gazed at the great bay. The breeze brought in a light fog, and smells of salt and fish wafted through the night air. With each wave, pilings creaked and groaned under the weight of the pier. San Diego was truly a paradise.

More time drifted by. Cassie's stomach growled for food. She hadn't eaten since morning.

More fog rolled in, and Cassie rubbed her arms

to ward off the chill. "You are cold?" a voice said out of the darkness.

Cassie stiffened. "Who—Felipe!"

Felipe stepped into her line of vision. How had he approached without a sound? He removed his tattered Army shirt and draped it over Cassie's shoulders. "I came as soon as I returned from my trip for game. I have no knowledge of what has happened except that you have been shot at. Do you know who is trying to kill you?"

Cassie wanted to hug Felipe for coming, but realized her hug might embarrass him in front of his Indian friend. "It's Will, the stuttering bandit who burned the wagon train. I know it's him."

"You are certain?"

Cassie nodded emphatically. For the next ten minutes she filled him in on the many things that had happened to her. "I think Will is afraid I'll have him arrested for burning the train."

"Can you prove it was him? I've heard much of Van Dyke, the old judge, since my return to the Springs. He does not hang a man without proof."

"How can we get proof?"

"You must go back to your uncle's ranch. Tell no one what you suspect, not even your uncle, until I find out more. I will meet you here tomorrow before sundown."

"I can't go back to the ranch. Will is there."

"Stay in your uncle's house and off the range. José will be nearby."

"Let me go with you, Felipe. More people will talk to us if I'm along."

"No, you will not be safe. Come here tomorrow night." He turned and whistled softly. His mount came obediently. "José will see you safely back to the ranch."

"But—" Cassie began. Felipe mounted his horse and was gone.

José handed Cassie Penny's reins. "Come, we go back to uncle."

"Oh, that Felipe, he always has to do everything himself. How will he know whom to talk to?"

José waited until Cassie mounted, then led the way. "He will know," was all he said.

Cassie and José traveled the short distance south to her uncle's ranch. At the road that led to the house, José reined in his horse. "I be near."

"How near? What if Will is waiting for me in the stable?"

"No stable. Leave horse at door."

When Cassie stepped into the entry, her uncle rushed from the parlor. "Where have you been?" he demanded. "It's dangerous for a young lady to be riding alone after dark. I sent a man to watch over you and he hasn't come back. Where is he?"

Suddenly embarrassed, and angry too, Cassie snapped at her uncle. "How should I know?" Then she apologized. "I'm sorry, Uncle Henry, I stayed too long at my friend's house. I didn't know it would get dark so fast."

"Well, you know now."

So Will hadn't returned. Had Felipe ambushed him somewhere along the way?

Uncle Henry seemed genuinely concerned for her safety. Had she misjudged him? Somehow she couldn't imagine the happy-go-lucky uncle she remembered doing anything to harm her.

Instead of going directly to her room, Cassie slipped down to the kitchen. She found Chin at the butcher-block table drinking tea. "Is there a spare cup of tea for me, and maybe some bread and cheese to go with it?"

Chin smiled. "You are hungry?"

"I'm starved. Somehow I missed dinner." She returned his smile. "And lunch."

Chin brought cheese and a crusty loaf of bread from the pantry, then filled her cup from the teapot on the table. "You have been in town all day?" he asked tentatively.

Felipe had cautioned her not to tell anyone about Will. She didn't. "This is a beautiful town. I was sightseeing and the quick twilight caught me in the dark."

Chin lowered his gaze and seemed to study his half-full cup of tea. Finally he raised his eyes. "Darkness holds many dangers. Be careful, Miss Cassie, when you ride alone."

CHAPTER THIRTEEN

*T*o Cassie, the next day seemed more like a week. Usually Will came to the ranch house at least once a day to confer with her uncle. This day he did not appear. Had Felipe attacked him? Maybe killed him? No, Felipe would not kill so easily. Will probably had no reason to come to the house.

The activity of ranch hands around the stable seemed unusually quiet. They were probably out on the range. Cassie scolded herself for being so suspicious. She could be wrong about Will; after all, she hadn't seen his face when the wagons were burned, only heard his voice after he had rummaged through her father's pockets. But he had followed her to the Valley of the Springs and tried to kill her; of that she was certain.

By afternoon she could stand it no longer. She left early to meet Felipe. "I'm going to visit my friend in town," she told Roberto, the young stable hand, when he saddled Penny. Roberto appeared to be fourteen, maybe fifteen, but he always smiled when Cassie came to the stable. He seemed to be

149

the one friendly face she had encountered on the ranch.

Today Roberto's smile was missing. He saddled Penny slowly, deliberately, as if his mind were elsewhere. When he handed her the reins his eyes clouded with worry. "Be careful," he said.

"Why? Tell me what's going on."

Roberto shook his head. "Be careful," he repeated.

On the short ride to town Cassie kept looking back along the road, expecting someone to follow her and hoping desperately that José was somewhere watching and protecting her. No one rode the trail behind her. Perhaps José had gone home, knowing she'd be safe in daylight. Did Roberto mean that she should be careful in town, or on the trail? Cassie wished she knew.

She briefly considered stopping to see Mary, but changed her mind. If trouble came, she didn't want Mary involved.

Instead, she stopped at a tea shop and found a table by the window. The heavenly aroma of fresh-baked bread filled the small cafe. A smiling waitress brought her tea and two slices of warm bread topped with melting butter. "You're new in town," she said. "Welcome to San Diego."

"I'm Cassie Harper. I've come to live with my uncle."

"Come see us again," the waitress said, and returned to her baking.

From her table by the window, Cassie watched

the busy street. Hammers sounded everywhere where new buildings were going up. Buckboards filled with fresh-cut lumber wobbled up the street. A carriage carrying a well-dressed woman stopped at a shop displaying hats in its window. This truly was a growing town.

Riders trotted their mounts down the street, obviously intent on business. Cassie scrutinized each rider, hoping that one might be Jason. None sat his horse as straight, or wore his wide-brimmed hat at the jaunty angle that Jason did. Had he forgotten her completely?

She swallowed the lump in her throat and forced her gaze away from the street. "If you ever need me . . ." he'd said. Well, she didn't need him. Felipe would help her learn if Will was one of the bandits.

Weeks ago she'd convinced herself that Jason couldn't be one of the bandits who had attacked the wagon train. Now new doubts crept into her mind. She pushed them away. She couldn't have fallen in love with a bandit.

There, she'd said it, if only to herself. She loved Jason Van Dyke, and she would trust him with her life.

The sun hovered on the horizon, and Cassie made her way to the pier on the waterfront. As the sun dropped out of sight, Cassie led Penny under the pier and tied her to a piling.

She leaned against the tall post and gazed at the bay. Small waves lapped at the sand, and fishing boats, their masts like black skeletons, rocked silently in the water. The aroma of salt air mixed with the dampness of incoming fog.

"You are alone? Where is José?" a voice asked from behind.

Cassie whirled. "Felipe, don't sneak up on me like that. I'm jumpy enough already. I haven't seen José."

"You have reason to be nervous. I have learned many things today."

"About Will?"

"Yes, but he will not bother you for a day or two."

"Did he burn the wagon train? Is that why he's trying to kill me?"

"He is a rustler." Felipe paused for several long moments before he went on. "Under the direction of your uncle, Will and the other hands on the ranch rustle herds of steers. They alter the brands, then drive them directly to the railroad. The sheriff has never been able to catch them, because when there is a witness, the witness is killed before he can testify."

Cassie gasped. "You mean my uncle kills people?"

Felipe went on. "It is not his usual business to attack wagon trains, but his entire ranch crew was away from the ranch at the time your train was attacked, and for several days after that. Also, four horses with the Van Dyke brand appeared on your uncle's ranch and then disappeared."

"No, I don't believe it. Jason is not a bandit!"

Felipe smiled at her outburst. "I believe the horses were rustled from the Van Dyke ranch. They beat up the old judge, but they didn't kill him. I would like to know why they let him live."

"Jason told me his father was beaten nearly to death."

"You've seen Jason?"

Cassie tried to keep the unhappiness out of her voice. "No, he told me that on the trail."

"I understand he's been asking questions in town."

"We'll never be able to prove that Will killed my father. I can't really identify anybody."

"You will have proof. Meet me here again tomorrow night. By then I will have something for you to take to the sheriff. Now I will take you back to your uncle's ranch."

"I can't go back there, now that I know about the rustling. What about José? Will he be there?"

Anger flashed across Felipe's face. "I fear José is dead."

"No!" Cassie cried. "They wouldn't dare just shoot a man!"

"If someone noticed him on the ranch, he would be shot as a trespasser."

A tear slipped down Cassie's cheek. "I didn't mean for anyone to die because of me."

Felipe untied Penny and motioned for Cassie to mount. "I will take you to the gate of your uncle's ranch. If there is trouble, go to Roberto—he is a friend. He will help you if he can. Tell no one what you know. You will be safe."

The house was dark when Chin let her in. "No one is home," he said. "Would you like some tea?"

Cassie followed him to the kitchen. While she ate, she felt Chin watching her. Did he know where she had been?

In the middle of the night she heard a commotion outside when her uncle and several of the ranch hands returned. Had they been in town for the night? They were noisy enough, laughing and calling to each other.

The next morning at breakfast, Uncle Henry seemed in good spirits. Cassie was glad she didn't have to account for coming in after dark.

To pass the time, she sat at her window, idly watching the sparse activity outside the stable. Two men loafed on a bench near the entrance. Once her uncle came out of the stable and talked with them, then came back to the house.

She had believed that Will wanted her dead because she could identify him as a bandit. But if Will worked for Uncle Henry. . . . She tried to remember all that she could of her uncle back in St. Louis, but there was not much she could recall from when she was ten.

She remembered her grandfather's anger at Uncle Henry. Once he had called him a dishonorable man. Cassie remembered asking her mother what that meant, and her mother's answer. "He's a thief. He should be sent to prison."

Cassie wondered what he had stolen, but soon after that, Uncle Henry went to California. "He is no longer a son of mine," her grandfather had declared, and Cassie had wondered how anybody could become not a son when he already was his son.

She remembered vividly her uncle's last words before he left. "I've been cheated by all of you."

Now she understood more. Obviously her uncle had stolen money from his father, and his father had disinherited him. That must be why her father had inherited all her grandfather's money, and maybe the reason he wouldn't spend it.

After lunch Cassie saddled Penny and left for town. She'd visit Mary, even though she'd promised herself she wouldn't. This time she'd be very careful that no one followed her. She'd feel better about Mary and the children when she knew John was back from his job on the fishing boat.

When she opened the door, Mary burst into tears. She pulled Cassie into the house. "What's going on?" she sobbed. "The day you were here, a man came here looking for you. He tried to force me to tell him where you had gone. I didn't know."

Cassie hugged Mary and sat her in a chair. "I didn't mean for you to get involved, that's why I didn't tell you. Oh, Mary, everything is so crazy at my uncle's ranch. I'm trying to find out who burned the wagon train." Cassie glanced around the room. "Where's John?"

"Someone from the dock brought me a message. He'll be gone two more days. Oh, I wish he'd come home. I'm frightened."

Cassie sat down beside Mary and took her hand. "So am I, but soon this will all be over." She longed to tell Mary that Felipe was helping her and that tonight she could go to the sheriff with evidence, but she had promised Felipe she would tell no one.

The baby cried and Cassie got to her feet. "If you see a stranger around, Mary, take the children and go to a neighbor. When John gets home, he'll take care of you."

Shortly before sundown, Cassie tied Penny to a piling under the pier.

Darkness came quickly, and as the minutes passed, a strange uneasiness enveloped Cassie. Every sound on the deserted beach startled her, stringing her nerves like a tightrope.

What must have been an hour passed. Still no Felipe. One at a time the stars blinked out, enveloped by fog. The cool night air chilled her bones. Where was Felipe?

Footsteps sounded on the pier overhead. Cassie huddled in the sand behind a piling. Penny pawed the sand, eager to go home. The footsteps receded. Whoever it was had walked out on the pier.

Out of the fog, a figure approached. He followed the shoreline to the pier. He studied her horse for several seconds. Fear nearly paralyzed her. Was he after her horse, or her? Cassie moved to grab the reins to show the horse was not alone. The man scooted away.

As the hours passed, the town became silent. Loud music no longer blared from the open door of the saloon. No longer did an occasional lone rider trot down the street. Still Felipe did not come.

He had promised he'd have proof of who had torched the wagon train and killed her father. Felipe would not let her wait alone in the darkness if he could get to her. He'd told her last night that he believed José was dead.

A whisper broke the quiet. "Cassie," the voice repeated.

When she turned, an Indian crouched no more than two feet away. She recognized him as one of the young braves who had been in the trees when Will shot at her. "Where is Felipe?" she asked urgently.

"Felipe gone," he said. "Three men beat him and drag him from uncle's stable."

Panic threatened to overwhelm her. "What was he doing at my uncle's stable? Where did they take him?"

The Indian shook his head. "I not know. Maybe kill him."

"I'll get Jason, he'll help. Where is Jason's ranch? How do I get there?"

The Indian shook his head again. "Not know."

Cassie mounted her horse and forced herself to guide Penny slowly along the waterfront. She had to think. Maybe Roberto could help her, but she dared not go home. If her uncle was guilty of sending his men after the wagon train, he'd find out where she had been, and why. He'd beat the truth out of her if that was the only way he could get it.

If Felipe needed help, she had to get it now. John was out to sea and the sheriff's office would be closed. That left only one person: Jason. If he didn't care about her, she knew he cared about Felipe. She remembered Jason's last words: *"If you ever need me, just ask for the Van Dyke place. Most anyone in town can tell you where it is."*

At this time of night, she had to find someone, anyone, who could tell her which road to take.

She ran out of beach and directed Penny back into the town. She walked her horse slowly up the main street, watching for someone to ask. Everything was closed, except for what appeared to be a card room. She drew Penny closer and peeked in the window. Dirty, unshaven men sat around a green-covered table, silently reaching for each card as it was dealt.

The front door opened. A woman's pink satin dress glistened in the light from inside. She stepped outside and leaned against the wall of the woodplank building. Cassie stopped. The woman looked up at her. "You lost, sister?"

"Can—can you tell me how to get to the Van Dyke ranch?"

The woman snickered. "Everybody knows where that is." She pointed southeast. "Go three corners up, then turn left. Follow that road maybe twenty miles up into the mountains. Can't miss it. It's a big house with a red roof, I hear." She squinted at Cassie. "You ain't aiming to ride there tonight, are you?"

Cassie let caution fly. "I have to," she said.

The woman shook her head. "You're a fool. You better move fast along the trail, it's no fittin' place for a woman to be alone."

"Thank you," Cassie said. "Thank you very much."

With a half salute, she waved Cassie away. "Good luck, kid, I hope you make it."

Cassie galloped Penny up the street and turned at the third corner. Ahead of her lay inky darkness. Here and there the shadowy form of a house appeared, but no lantern light showed through a window.

Soon there were no more houses, just a narrow trail bordered by dry grass and an occasional live oak tree. She glanced back at the fog she'd left behind. Above her, stars twinkled in the sky, and the moon outlined the trail.

On and on she galloped, looking back often to make certain no one followed her. The woman had warned her to move fast. Every time Cassie neared a tree close to the trail, she tensed, half expecting one of her uncle's men to jump out.

Up ahead, covered with trees, the mountains loomed darkly, reminding her of the danger that could lie ahead. She could run Penny on level ground, but when they got to the mountains, the going would be slow.

She halted Penny near a clump of trees and dismounted to give the horse a rest. Hidden by the trees, she studied the moonlit trail behind her. If she were being followed, he'd have to show himself on the long unprotected stretch of trail. She saw no one.

She patted her horse, then laid her cheek against the warm shoulder. "I don't know what's up in those hills, Penny, but we have to go up there and find Jason."

Penny bobbed her head in agreement. Cassie looked both ways on the trail before she emerged from the trees, then mounted up and headed into the mountains.

Up and up they went. The trees turned from live oak to pine, and the cold night air cut through the sleeves of her thin silk blouse.

An hour into the woods, Cassie heard hoofbeats behind her. Someone was coming fast up the trail. She jumped to the ground and pulled Penny off the trail into the dense forest. She waited in breath-holding silence, her hand ready to cover Penny's muzzle if she threatened to make a sound.

Cassie tensed. Fear threatened to tear her to pieces. She felt for her gun. It gave her a small measure of security.

Finally the rider galloped by. She squinted to see him clearly. He didn't have Will's thick build, and for that she was grateful.

She waited until the hoofbeats receded into the distance. Still, she dared not go ahead. The rider could stop and ambush her.

Her hands trembled when at last she mounted Penny and guided her back onto the trail. She had to go on. If Felipe were being tortured for information, he'd die before he'd tell. Jason would help her find him.

Cassie rode doggedly on, hoping at every turn to see the big white house she was looking for. She studied the starlit sky between the branches above her. It had to be at least three in the morning.

Fear held her rigidly alert to every sound. She heard trickling water and stopped at a stream for Penny to drink. A light breeze blew strands of her hair across her face, and she realized it had become unpinned and lay tangled on her shoulders. She smiled to herself. Jason would recognize her. She looked much as she had the last time he'd seen her. Only the urgency of the night kept her from crying.

A coyote howled, then another. At first she paid little attention. Then memory shook her. The hostile Indians in the desert had used that signal.

She slapped Penny's rump and galloped up the trail. Overhanging branches slapped at her face. She leaned forward against Penny's neck to avoid their reach. She had to get to Jason.

Ahead, a clearing stretched before her. She reined in Penny at the edge. There it was, far in the distance: the big white house she'd been searching for, Jason's house. Once more she urged Penny into a gallop and covered the long lane to the front door.

She slipped to the ground and ran up the steps. With all her strength she pounded on the enormous oak door. "Wake up, Jason," she yelled. "Let me in."

She pounded until her fists ached, then leaned sobbing against the door. When it finally opened she would have fallen inside, but a gray-haired man kept her from falling.

"Jason, I want Jason," she cried. "I'm Cassie, please let me in."

The old man half-closed the door, keeping her outside. "I don't know any Cassie."

"Please," she sobbed. "Let me inside. I'm Henry Harper's niece from San Diego. I have to find Jason."

"He's not here, and I want no part of Hank Harper's kin." He pushed at the door to close it.

Cassie's sobs turned to anger. She pushed back with all her strength, but she couldn't budge the old man. "You— You stinking bandit!" she yelled. "Let me in!"

The door slammed shut and Cassie heard the bolt slip into place. She stood on the steps in the dark, once more alone.

CHAPTER FOURTEEN

*H*alf an hour later, darkness shrouded Jason and his horse as he made his way from the south to the rear of the ranch house. He'd picked up a lot of disturbing information from a group of his friends on the American side of the Mexican border.

He'd learned that the four horses rustled from his ranch the night his father was beaten had appeared in a small Mexican village, twenty miles south of the border. The brands had obviously been changed, but his friends swore they were Van Dyke brands.

He had also learned they'd been sold cheap by two of Hank Harper's ranch hands. They had wanted to get rid of them at any price. He was told that Harper and his whole crew had spent more than a week in the desert. In Jason's mind that put Hank Harper right in the middle of the rustling and possibly the burning of Cassie's wagon train.

Nothing could bring back the wagon train, and his horses could be replaced. But Cassie was in her uncle's house. Jason's head pounded with anger and frustration. He had to get her out of there.

He led his stallion into the stable and removed the saddle. First he had to tell his father that proof of Hank Harper's rustling was impossible to get. Nobody was willing to tell what he knew in court.

Pedro came from his room and grabbed the reins. "I will feed him, Papa Jason."

"I'll take care of him, Pedro, go back to bed. A young man needs a full night's sleep."

Pedro insisted. "I will do it. You are tired, and your face is very dirty."

Jason smiled tiredly. "So my face is dirty. Guess I'll have to do something about that."

Jason entered the house, surprised that a lamp still burned on the table. His father dozed in his big leather chair. That wasn't like the old judge. "Did you forget to go to bed?"

The judge jerked awake when Jason spoke. "I was waiting for you. There was a—"

Jason interrupted before the judge could finish his sentence. "I located our horses. They were sold in a Mexican village by two of Harper's men. But I have no proof." Jason dropped into a chair and leaned his head back. "Even the Mexicans know that Harper kills witnesses." Jason got up and headed for the kitchen. "I've got to eat and go to San Diego."

The old judge attempted to follow him but fell back in his chair. "Not until you sleep. From the looks of you, you haven't done much of that in the past forty-eight hours."

By now Jason was halfway down the hall. His father called after him. "There was a girl here, maybe you can find her and get her to talk. She's Harper's niece."

Jason raced back to his father and grabbed his shoulders. "Where is she? I've got to find her."

The old judge pulled loose from his son's grip. "How should I know? I told her to get out of here. I want no part of Hank Harper's kin."

"Cassie!" Jason grabbed his gunbelt and ran out the door.

His father yelled after him. "You didn't eat— You forgot your hat."

In the stable, Jason slapped a saddle on his mount, leaped into it, and galloped down the road toward San Diego. Anger and anxiety pushed him faster—anger at his father for sending Cassie away, and fear that one of Harper's men had followed Cassie and might attack her.

Cassie had come to him for help and the judge had turned her away. "Cassie," he groaned. "Where are you?"

Still fuming at Jason's father, Cassie stopped at a small clearing by a stream. She had only intended to rest Penny and let her graze for a few minutes, but Cassie was so tired. . . .

Certain she heard wolves, she built a small fire to keep them at bay. She tossed a few more twigs on the fire. If she waited for daylight to follow the trail back to San Diego, the going would be faster.

She sat cross-legged by the fire, her pistol handy in her lap. If anyone or anything tried to attack her, she felt angry enough to shoot to kill.

Elbow on one knee, chin cupped in her hand, she gazed into the fire. The question of who had kidnapped Felipe and why kept spinning around in her head. He had told her that he would have proof she could take to the sheriff. What kind of proof could he possibly have? It must be something that would place her uncle and his men at the burning of the wagon train, but what?

Another witness? Who would be brave enough to testify against Henry Harper and his gang? She would, but she hadn't actually seen Will's face, only heard his voice.

Over the past hours, Cassie had come to realize that the wagon train had been burned solely to kill her and her father. Did her father carry a threat to his brother? No. Her father was not a man to hold a grudge. He loved Uncle Henry. Cassie suspected that that was the reason her father had refused to spend his inheritance. He had wanted to share it with Uncle Henry.

She wondered if her uncle knew that. If he didn't and he still felt cheated. . . . Of course, that was it! By killing her father, Uncle Henry would inherit the money, unless Cassie was still alive to be the heir.

Tears ran down her cheeks as she gazed sadly into the fire. Her father had died for nothing.

A twig snapped, then another. Cassie jerked to attention. She aimed her gun toward the sound. "Stop right there or I'll kill you," she yelled.

The sound came closer. Cassie aimed. "I mean it. I'll kill you."

A man's figure stopped at the edge of her clearing, not twenty feet from her. He leaned insolently against a big pine. "Stop, I said!"

"You're a dangerous woman, no matter where I find you," the voice said.

Cassie let out her breath with a whoosh. "Jason! I could have shot you."

Cassie laid her gun on the ground, and Jason came to sit beside her. He tried to conceal the enormous relief that washed over him. "What's happened, Cassie?"

Her words tumbled out one over the other. "Uncle Henry or somebody has kidnapped Felipe. Maybe he's dead, I don't know, but we have to find him. And I know why Uncle Henry killed my father, and now he's trying to kill me. Felipe promised to meet me and give me proof. I waited and waited. He didn't come. Then a friend of Felipe's, an Indian, came and told me three men grabbed Felipe at my uncle's ranch."

Jason's arm encircled her shoulders and he pulled her close. "Calm down, Cassie. Tell me everything you know."

Cassie brushed a hand across her eyes and

poured out her thoughts. "I know that's why Will tried to kill me. My uncle ordered him to do it to get my father's inheritance."

Jason groaned in disbelief. "How could a man kill his own brother for anything as unimportant as money? But then, Harper is a greedy man." He didn't speak for several moments, and Cassie didn't interrupt his thoughts. Then he went on. "I wonder what Felipe had as proof. Do you think he saw the attack on the wagon train?"

"I don't know, he didn't tell me anything, just said he'd have proof I could take to the sheriff."

"Then it has to be something else. An Indian's word wouldn't carry much weight in court."

Cassie jumped to her feet. "We have to find Felipe before they kill him, whether he has any proof or not. He came to help me when I had nobody else."

"First we go back to my place and eat. I'd guess you haven't had a bite since morning."

"But that will take precious time. Felipe could be dying."

"Trying to find food in the mountains will take more time."

"Felipe is being held captive in town. I know he is."

Jason helped Cassie mount Penny. "I think he's in the mountains. If Felipe has evidence that could hang Harper, I doubt that your uncle would risk having him discovered."

"Maybe he's holding Felipe prisoner on the ranch. The ranch hands are loyal to my uncle."

"You can't be sure of that. I have friends south of here who may know something."

Cassie's stomach growled from hunger. "I guess we'd better eat first."

At the door of the ranch house, Pedro smiled broadly when he took their horses. Maybe it was because Jason was smiling.

Cassie followed Jason through the front door. The old judge sat in a big chair, a cane resting beside him. Jason brought Cassie forward. "I found her. We'll leave soon as we eat."

The old man didn't answer, looking the other way, as if Cassie didn't exist.

In the kitchen Leo fried eggs and potatoes and set them before the two travelers. Then he added big wedges of warm bread and churned butter. While they ate, Jason told Cassie what he had learned about her uncle and his ranch hands, and about his stolen horses too.

Cassie ate everything served to her and washed it down with fragrant coffee. She watched Jason as he ate, but lowered her gaze when he looked her way. She noticed Leo grin.

Jason motioned to Leo. "We need food for a day or two to take with us. Bread, cheese, anything you can pack quickly."

"You're leaving now?"

"Yes, it's almost daylight."

Once more astride the horses, Cassie and Jason

headed south. They rode for most of an hour before Jason led her to a small cabin in the forest. A grizzled man answered his knock and invited them in.

Jason didn't bother with formalities. "Have you seen anyone, maybe three or four men leading an Indian, come through in the night? Could have been yesterday in daylight."

The old man nodded. "Went east. Likely to the desert."

Cassie groaned aloud. "We'll never find him in the desert. He could be anyplace!"

"Not far," the man said. "They come back without the Indian this morning, early."

"They couldn't reach the desert in that length of time," Cassie said.

Jason agreed. "This far south they could reach the high desert. There's caves in the hills, and old mines. Thank you, my friend."

They traveled east and Cassie welcomed the warm sun against her face. The light breeze blew her hair across her cheek. She brushed it aside. In daylight, with Jason beside her, the trees no longer looked ominous, nor the trail too narrow to follow.

Jason glanced back at her, then slowed his mount until he rode beside her. He watched her for a long moment as she tried to twist her hair into a dignified bun on her neck, then grinned when she shrugged and let it fall. "Leave it alone, I like it that way," he said.

Frustrated, Cassie snapped at him. "You've never seen it any other way."

He gazed at her several seconds. "Yes, I have. I saw you in town on your way into the tea shop. I must admit, you looked quite elegant."

Hurt that he hadn't stopped, but pleased that he'd seen her in something besides a trail-dusty split skirt and a smudged silk blouse, she answered him pertly. "Why didn't you come in and at least say hello?"

"A couple of Harper's men were on the street. I didn't think it wise. Harper and his bunch don't care much for my father—or me. Next week your uncle must come to court on a serious assault charge. My father will be the judge. I think that may be why his men beat my father but didn't kill him. To warn him."

"So Uncle Henry will go free."

Jason straightened in his saddle. "He will not go free if he's guilty. Not in my father's court."

"What if they kill him next time?"

"He'll take that chance."

"Stubborn old coot, isn't he?"

Jason grinned. "That he is."

The sound of horses echoed in the distance. Jason grabbed Cassie's horse and backed into the trees.

Two riders, their mounts glistening with sweat, raced by.

"Bandits," Jason said. "Nobody familiar. Probably just coming through."

"At a gallop?"

"Bandits have little consideration for their

horses. I doubt that there's any connection between them and Felipe."

Jason and Cassie rode on and on. They stopped around noon to eat and rest the horses. When Jason helped her remount, his hands circled her waist. For several seconds she stood mesmerized by the sensation of her back pressed against his long, lean body.

Suddenly he hoisted her into her saddle without waiting for her to get a foot in the stirrup. "We'll never find Felipe standing around here," he said.

By nightfall they had searched a dozen caves and one abandoned mine. Far in the distance, across a canyon, more caves dotted the sandy hill. "Can they wait until morning?" Cassie asked. "I don't know how much longer I can stay awake."

Jason helped her to the ground, and once more his hands lingered on her waist. This time he looked long into her eyes before he turned away abruptly. "I think we've come too far. The hermit said the riders were back early in the morning. Wherever Felipe is hidden, we've missed him."

Early the next morning, a dozen circling vultures swooped around and around in the sky. Jason studied them, then pointed to a deep canyon. "The buzzards are waiting for something to die, something larger than a jackrabbit. Maybe a coyote."

Ripples of heat emanated from the sand in the bushy ravine, reminding Cassie of the awful heat when they had crossed the desert. "Or a man."

"Or a man," Jason echoed and kicked his horse into a run. Cassie followed, urging Penny into a gallop.

At the edge of the ravine, Jason slid from his mount and, half running, led him down.

Cassie came close behind him. Coarse brush pulled at her skirt and gouged her legs as she tried to keep up with Jason. Behind her, Penny followed her lead.

At the bottom of the canyon, the buzzards circled back and forth. "Over there!" Jason shouted, reaching for Cassie's hand to hurry her along behind him.

Scratching their way through low brush covered with tiny round stickers, they found a small sandy clearing. Bound spread-eagle on the sand in the torrid desert heat trapped by the canyon, Felipe lay unconscious. Dried blood was caked in grotesque patterns across his bruised body.

Cassie reached him first. She laid her head on his scorched chest. "Felipe, Felipe," she cried. He didn't move.

Jason uncapped his canteen and wet Felipe's face, then his chest. "He's still alive. Help me untie him." Jason pulled a hunting knife from a sheath on his belt and sawed at the rawhide binding.

Cassie struggled with the bands on Felipe's ankles. "I can't get them loose."

Jason leaped to her side and cut the bands that held Felipe's feet. Felipe still didn't move.

"Are you sure he's alive?" Tears spilled down Cassie's cheeks.

"He's breathing, but we have to get him out of the sun." Carefully he lifted Felipe into his arms. "Get the horses. I'll carry him up."

Cassie grabbed the reins of Penny and Jason's stallion and followed Jason up the steep bank of the ravine. At the top, he laid Felipe in the shade of a live oak. Still he didn't stir.

"Felipe, wake up," Cassie cried. "Please, don't die."

Jason ripped a swath of cloth from his own shirt-tail. He held it toward Cassie. "Water," he ordered.

Cassie poured from her canteen until water dribbled onto Felipe's chest. She watched anxiously while Jason sponged Felipe's face. Tears ran down her cheeks. If Felipe died, it would be her fault.

Felipe's eyes opened. When he looked toward Jason, what appeared to be a huge sigh of relief shook his body. "The letter," he whispered, "get the letter. . . . Take to . . . sheriff. . . ."

"What letter?" Cassie cried. "Where is it?"

Felipe tried to sit up, reaching for the water. Jason tipped his canteen against Felipe's swollen lips. "Just a sip or two."

Minute by minute Felipe seemed to gain strength, until he sat up on his own. "I am very hungry," he said.

Cassie handed him a wedge of bread. He chewed several small pieces, washing them down with sips of water.

Cassie's patience exploded. "What letter are you talking about? I don't have any letter."

Felipe shook his head as if to drive the fog away. "Before Will and the others captured me, I slipped it to Chin. He is your friend."

"What's in the letter that can convict Hank Harper?"

"I don't know. The letter was sealed. I found it in Will's mattress in the bunkhouse. On the envelope I read, 'If I am killed, give this to the sheriff. Hank Harper ain't going to get away with murder.'"

"How did you know about the letter?" Jason asked.

"A friend brought me a message from Chin." Felipe smiled weakly at Cassie. "The old houseman thinks you are a fine lady."

Jason helped Felipe to his feet. "Can you ride?"

Felipe swayed with his first steps, but then headed for Jason's big stallion. "We must be careful going down. I believe Will and his friends will be back to see if I am ready to tell them where I put the letter. They will not kill me until they know."

Felipe leaned heavily against Jason's back as he rode behind him down the mountain. Cassie followed close behind as Jason led her through the pines. This was his territory; he knew every path in these mountains. He'd spent a lifetime in them, dodging renegades and bandits.

Twice they stopped to let the horses and Felipe

rest. By now, in spite of the thick welts on his chest and back, the Indian seemed almost recovered from the fierce beating he'd taken.

When they finally came within sight of her uncle's ranch, they stopped in a clump of oak trees. Cassie slid from Penny's back and joined Felipe and Jason. "I'm going in alone," she said firmly. "I'll find Chin and get the letter."

Jason grabbed her shoulders. "They'll kill you. I won't let you go," Jason said. "I won't let you go in there without protection."

"Then cover me from here. You can't just walk in the front door and look for Chin. You don't know your way around my uncle's house. Somebody will shoot you and say you were trespassing. Nobody will pay any attention when I walk in."

Jason was adamant until Felipe interrupted. "She is right. It's the only way to fool Will and Harper."

For just a second, Cassie enjoyed the reluctance in Jason's eyes. Reluctance and something more. Love? But the fear diffused her enjoyment quickly. If Will suspected she had found Felipe, he would kill her without hesitation.

The worry in Jason's eyes reminded her she could be riding into a death trap. "One hour," he said brusquely. "If you aren't back in one hour, I'm coming in after you."

Before Jason could say more, she leaped into the saddle and raced for the ranch, slowing when she reached the entrance to the Harper property. Step by slow step she guided Penny down the long lane that led to the ranch house.

Fear alerted every nerve in her body. She felt for her gun. It would be a poor defense against a rifle. With all her strength she held Penny to a walk. A man crossed the ranch yard and disappeared. Another followed. He disappeared too.

Cassie rode on, closer and closer to the ranch house. Her heart thudded with fear. *Don't panic,* she told herself. *Just don't panic and go galloping in. If you do, you're dead.*

CHAPTER FIFTEEN

*P*erspiration dampened Cassie's forehead and trickled down the side of her face. She wiped it away with her shoulder, not daring to let go of the reins. She felt eyes from the ranch watching her. Was one of those eyes sighting down the barrel of a rifle?

She went on down the lane. Forty yards, thirty yards to go. She moved closer and closer to the front door of the ranch house.

Her hair hung in a tangled mass on her shoulders. Her white silk blouse, smudged and wrinkled, would tell anyone she'd been riding most of the night.

Step by step she guided Penny ahead. The massive oak door of the house loomed before her. She halted Penny and slid to her feet.

The stable boy hurried from the stable and took Penny's reins. He looked at Cassie curiously but didn't speak. She wanted to tell him not to take her horse, that she'd need it again in a few minutes, but she dared not arouse suspicion.

The steps to the wide veranda felt like the steps to the gallows. Cassie's knees trembled. If her uncle or Will suspected that she knew who had the envelope and that she had come to get it, she would be killed without mercy and buried in some remote, unmarked grave on the ranch. Cassie shuddered.

With courage she didn't know she had, she opened the door, walked through the entry, and went up the stairs. Inside her room she leaned against the closed door and let out her breath with a swoosh.

Her mind worked overtime planning how to get the letter from Chin and get back to Jason and Felipe. She opened her bedroom door and listened. She heard nothing.

Slowly she made her way down the stairs to Chin's kitchen. He jumped nervously when she spoke. "Chin," she whispered, "I've come for the letter. Felipe and Jason are waiting in the trees beyond the lane."

Some of the anxiety left Chin's face. "Felipe is alive?"

"We found him in the desert. He will be fine."

"Come, I get letter."

Cassie followed him into the pantry. For several seconds he dug in a big sack of flour; then he pulled out a smudged envelope. He wiped off the flour and handed the envelope to Cassie. "Take care," he said.

Cassie nodded. "I'm going out the back door. I

hope nobody sees me head across the field. Jason and Felipe are waiting for me in a clump of trees."

"Wait for dark, Miss Cassie. You will be safer."

"I can't. If I don't return in an hour, Jason will come in after me."

He must have sensed her urgency because he led her to the back door and pointed. "Follow that fence line and you will not be seen from the barnyard."

She tucked the letter firmly inside her shirt. She frowned. "How is it that you know Felipe well enough for him to trust you with this?"

Chin displayed a rare smile. "When Felipe was a boy, I worked in the kitchen of the rich Englishman who raised him. We became friends. Last week he asked me to watch over you and to listen for trouble." Chin shrugged. "In the stable I heard Will bragging that he had a letter that could—how did he say it?—nail Harper to the wall."

"And Felipe got caught in the bunkhouse looking for it."

"He slipped it to me in the stable before the ranch hands grabbed him."

Chin opened the kitchen door. He glanced in both directions, then motioned Cassie to leave. "Take care," he repeated.

She scooted out the door, staying close to the back of the house until she knew she could not be seen from the barnyard and stable. Eyeing the line of fence, she ran as fast as she could, glancing back every few steps.

On and on she ran, stumbling over the rough terrain. Once she fell to the ground. She struggled to her feet and ran on. In the distance she could see the clump of trees that hid Jason and Felipe. It seemed a mile away.

She heard hoofbeats. Was somebody following her? She dropped to the ground and glanced back. In the distance, someone galloped along the lane, headed for the entrance. A ranch hand going to town? Or looking for her? She was too far away to recognize the rider.

When the horseman went through the gate toward town, she got to her feet and ran for the trees. Fifty more yards, forty, ten. . . . She ran headlong into Jason's arms. He held her against him as if he'd never let her go. "I got it," she sobbed against his shoulder. "I got the letter."

Cassie handed him the letter. He tucked it into his shirt. "We'll take it right to the sheriff."

"Aren't you going to open it?" Cassie asked indignantly. "I risked my life for that thing. I'd like to know what's in it."

Jason's arm circled her shoulders. "I know you did, darling, but I'd rather not tamper with evidence. It's up to the sheriff to tell us what's in it."

Cassie didn't answer. All she heard was *"darling."* Her heart thudded. He'd called her darling!

Felipe brought Jason's stallion forward. "We have only one horse. I'll walk. I must return to my people in the Valley of the Springs. They are worried that I am dead."

"You are too weak to walk so far," Jason said. "You'll take the stallion."

Felipe did not argue. He mounted the stallion. "Be careful when you enter the town," he warned them. "You are not safe until you have delivered the letter to the sheriff."

Hand in hand, Jason and Cassie walked the few short blocks to the sheriff's office. When Jason handed him the letter, he read the message on the envelope, then tore it open. A crumpled map, folded inside a note, fell to the desk. Cassie picked it up. "This belonged to my father. It came from Uncle Henry, giving directions on how to get to his ranch."

The sheriff nodded, then read the accompanying note aloud. " 'Under orders from Hank Harper to burn the wagon train and everybody on it, I took this map from his dead brother's pocket.' "

Cassie's eyelids burned, but she held back the tears that threatened to fall. The stuttering bandit had taken double eagles from her father's pockets, but because her head had been hidden under the shawl, she didn't know he'd found the map too.

The sheriff folded the papers together and replaced them in the envelope. "This should convict Will *and* Harper of murder." Anger crossed his face. "I've been after Harper for a long time. We'll have him and Will behind bars in an hour, I guarantee it."

The sheriff glanced at Cassie. "Where are you

going to go? You can't go back to Harper's ranch. There could be a lot of shooting."

Jason hesitated too long before he spoke. "I'll . . . I'll take her home with me."

Outside, the afternoon sun glistened like a ball of fire in the sky. She wanted to go home with Jason—she'd go anywhere with him—but not because he felt sorry for her. "No, I won't go home with you. I'll stay in San Diego and get a job."

"Doing what?" He grinned. "Somehow I can't imagine you fitting in with the saloon girls."

Cassie stepped away from him indignantly. "I'm a teacher. I'll teach the children in town to read and write. Anyway, I can't go to your house. I called your father a stinking bandit."

Jason grinned. "I have an idea he's been called worse than that, and by people not as pretty as you. With a little time, he'll learn to love you—the way I do."

Words stuck in Cassie's throat. He said he loved her. She found her voice. "Then why don't you ask me to marry you?"

Jason's startled face tempted her to laugh, but she didn't.

He pulled her into his arms right in the middle of downtown San Diego in broad daylight. He kissed her soundly. "That's what I plan to do, as soon as we get back to the judge." He held her close and kissed the tip of her ear. "Or would you prefer a preacher?"

B. W.